The Pretender

Even the book morphs!
Flip the pages
and check it out!

Look for other **ANIMORPHS**®
titles by K.A. Applegate:

the andalite chronicles

The Hork-Bajir Chronicles

The Pretender

K.A. Applegate

AN
APPLE
PAPERBACK

SCHOLASTIC INC.
New York Toronto London Auckland Sydney
Mexico City New Delhi Hong Kong

Cover illustration by David B. Mattingly

ISBN 0-590-76256-7

12 11 10 9 8 7 6 5 4 3 2 1   8 9/9 0 1 2 3/0

Printed in the U.S.A.   40

First Scholastic printing, November 1998

The author would like to thank Michael Mates

for his help in preparing this manuscript.

For Tonya Alicia Martin

Also for Michael and Jake

The Pretender

CHAPTER 1

My name is Tobias.

That's my name. But names don't really tell you much, do they? I've known two Rachels. One was this whiny, obnoxious person. The other Rachel — the one I know now — is the bravest person I've ever known.

But you'd think that my telling you my name is Tobias would at least tell you that I'm human, wouldn't you? You'd assume I have arms and legs and a face and a mouth. But names don't even tell you that.

I am not human.

I was human once. I was born a human. There are human characteristics within me. And I can become a human for two hours at a time. But I am not human.

I am a red-tailed hawk. A very common species of hawk, nothing exotic. Red-tails tend to live in woods near an open field or meadow. We hunt best that way: by sitting on a tree branch, gazing out across the field, spotting prey, then swooping in quickly for the kill.

That's what I do. I live in the trees near a very nice meadow. Unfortunately, the hunting has been bad lately. Partly that's just the way it goes. There are good times and bad times in the preda- tor business.

But more, it's competition. Another red-tail has been moving in on my territory. He's been eating my mice. Between him and the minor drought we've been having, food's getting a little scarce.

Stupid, huh? Stupid that I'd worry about something like that. I mean, I have powers far greater than that other red-tail. I can morph to human. I can morph to any animal. I could morph to some member of the feline family or some kind of snake and take out the red-tail.

Only I don't.

I could confront the other hawk. Red-tail to red-tail. We could fight it out.

Only I don't.

I don't do anything. Pretty soon he'll make a

move on me, push me aside. Maybe then I'll have to figure out what to do. But right now, I don't do anything. I just go hungry.

I could go to the others for help. To Rachel and the other Animorphs, my friends. But how weak is that? How can I go begging for help to deal with a situation I should be able to handle myself?

I sat on my branch, in my tree, and watched the dry grass. I watched as only a hawk can watch. With telescope eyes and a mind that never grows tired of looking for the clues to a kill.

I waited and watched and listened. A twitch of a grass stalk. A slight puff of rising dust. The faint sounds of tiny feet scrabbling in the dirt.

And from time to time I looked across the meadow at him. At the other hawk. He was a hundred yards away. The length of a football field. But I could see him clearly. It was like looking in a far-distant mirror. The angry, yellow-brown eyes. The wickedly curved beak. The sharp talons dug into the bark of a branch.

He looked at me. Our eyes met. He was pure hawk. I was . . . I was that unique, misfit creature called Tobias.

<No,> I said to him, though of course he understood nothing. <No, I won't use my morphing powers against you. It will be me and you. Hawk against hawk.>

He returned his gaze to the field. So did I. I had long since marked the burrow of a rabbit and its family. Three baby rabbits had survived. I was human enough to know that people — humans — would be disgusted by the sight of my killing and eating a baby rabbit. They would rather I at least go after the adult female.

But they'd be wrong. Life in the meadow isn't a Disney movie. If I killed the mother, the babies would all die. If I killed only the baby, the mother would survive to breed again.

Breed more babies for me to take. To rip apart. To eat.

There was another consideration: Rabbits are tougher than mice. They can aim those powerful hind legs and deliver a blow that will knock you silly.

This is my life. A meadow running short of prey. A competitor who would like to push me out altogether. And a family of rabbits who had to die so that I could live.

See what I mean about names not telling you very much? In the old days, back when I was truly human, "Tobias" was a word that meant wimp. That's what I was. I guess I was a nice person, back then. I guess teachers liked me and girls felt sorry for me. But the bullies were drawn to me like a mosquito to a sweaty neck.

That all changed in the most unexpected way you can possibly imagine. It changed on the night Jake, Rachel, Marco, Cassie, and I went walking through the abandoned construction site.

That's where we saw the damaged spacecraft land. That's where we met the doomed Andalite prince. Elfangor.

It was Elfangor who told us that our lives as we'd known them were going to end. Had already ended. He told us about the secret Yeerk invasion of Earth. An intimate invasion by the parasite slugs who enter your brain and enslave you.

And it was Elfangor who gave us powers no one but an Andalite had ever had before. It was Elfangor who transformed us with Andalite morphing technology.

We gained the ability to touch an animal, absorb its DNA, and then to *become* that animal.

Yes, to become.

I morphed a hawk. I overstayed the two-hour time limit. I was trapped. Trapped in the body of a red-tailed hawk.

Trapped in a world where another bird can be a dangerous enemy. Trapped in a world where I must kill to eat. And not like humans do, where they hire someone else to draw the blood and shatter the bone and then get the food in sanitized plastic packages at the supermarket.

I must kill my own food. I must swoop down and drive the sharp talons into the brain, into the neck. I must feel the heart stop beating. After . . . after I have already begun to feed.

That's what the name Tobias means. For this Tobias. For this one, strange, unique creature.

Movement!

Just a slight twitch of a single grass stalk. I looked at my opponent. He had not seen it.

This kill was mine.

I opened my wings, caught the breeze, and swooped down low across the reaching wildflowers and waving yellow grass.

Swooooosh!

I saw the flash of brown. I saw the small rabbit. I was intensely focused. I was electrified.

It happened in seconds.

I spilled air, changed the angle of attack, flipped my tail to aim, and dropped, talons wide open, onto the baby rabbit.

It didn't see me!

Its mother did, but she was three feet away. Too far!

In seconds my talons would close . . .

<Aaaahhhh!>

Suddenly, I was scared, helpless, frozen with terror! Above me the wings blotted out the sun. Huge, monstrous talons came down, like they were reaching down from the sky itself.

I screamed in terror. I plowed into the ground, beak first. I was a hawk again. But I had hit the dirt, missing my prey.

I flapped madly, panicked. I tried to catch air, then . . .

FWAPP!

Two big rabbit legs kicked and hit me across the side of my head, snapping my head back so fast I almost blacked out.

There was dust in my eyes. I blinked, frantic, terrified. I saw the baby rabbit hopping away. I saw the mother rabbit keeping station between it and me. The mother gaped at me with one perfectly round eye. Her mouth worked, her ears twitched.

She did not see the second shadow. The one that came up from behind her, dropped, opened its talons, and flew away, dragging her baby to its death.

CHAPTER 2

I was still hungry. And now I was shaken up, too. This was not the first time I'd had a similar experience. It had started in the last couple of weeks. Weird flashes like waking dreams. I would be closing in on my prey and then, in that ultimate moment, I would feel my mind transferred into that prey.

At least that's how it felt. I know it sounds crazy. But then, if you're me, how can you even talk about crazy and sane?

Sometimes I wonder if the truth is that I'm some lunatic. I wonder if in reality I'm a hopeless, raving madman locked in an asylum, merely imagining that I am a hawk.

8

Maybe I'm wearing a straitjacket. Maybe I'm in a padded room in a row of other padded rooms full of nuts who think they're Napoleon or George Washington or a red-tailed hawk.

How would I know? Does a madman know he's mad? Does he realize that the delusion isn't real?

I left the rabbit to the other hawk. But that indelible memory of being the prey instead of the predator hung over me, shadowed my mind. Even with the bright early-morning sun baking up thermals off the roads and parking lots, I felt like I was flying in shadow.

But there was a stronger need than the need for sanity. I was hungry. Hungry in that desperate, all-consuming way a predator has. It's a mean hunger. A dangerous hunger.

It was early still. The housing development below me was quiet. Parents were getting into their cars and driving off to work. Kids were waiting for buses. Some were talking or playing around. Most were standing glumly, wiping the sleep out of their eyes.

I floated above it all, ignored by the humans below me. And then I saw it.

It was fresh, I could see that right away. A raccoon, its back quarter smashed flat by a tire.

Roadkill. Carrion.

But it was fresh. It hadn't been dead more than an hour. The flesh would still be warm, especially on this warm day. But the maggots would not have started growing. Not yet.

I circled above it.

If only it had still been breathing. Stupid, isn't it? Drawing a line between prey that's alive, that you have to kill, and somehow pretending that's okay, that's right. And on the other hand, acting like something already dead is off-limits.

The truth is, I'd seen hawks eat roadkill. Older, weaker hawks. Unlucky hawks. It happens.

It just hadn't happened to me.

I circled lower. So fresh. I was so hungry. Such a stupid, meaningless distinction. My hunger argued with me. My hunger was convincing.

I dropped down, as suddenly as if I were going in for the kill. Maybe I wanted to pretend that's what I was doing.

I dropped down and landed on cracked blacktop. I looked around for cars. The street was empty.

Quickly, furtively, I ripped my beak into the raccoon's belly. And I began to feed.

Yes, it was still warm. I gobbled. I ripped and swallowed. Ripped and swallowed.

"Tobias?"

I snapped my head around, but I had already recognized the voice.

Rachel? No! Oh, God, no! No.

She just stood there, schoolbooks under her arm. Rachel would be beautiful in the middle of mud slides and hailstorms. On a sweet, sunny day, she made my heart ache.

She looked at me. Embarrassed for me. Wanting to say something that would make it all right. Not knowing what to say. Hurting for me. Feeling my humiliation.

What could I do?

I flapped my wings, skimmed across the pavement, and finally soared into the air.

She might believe I was some other hawk. She might. Or at least she would pretend to.

A piece of raccoon liver was in my mouth. I swallowed it.

11

CHAPTER 3

I saw Rachel again two days later. I'd checked in with Jake to see if anything was going on. There were no missions — we'd worked plenty lately, dealing with the horrifying matter of David, the first new Animorph.

David had ended up like me, as what the Andalites call a *nothlit*. A person trapped in morph. But David had been trapped in the body of a rat. No flying for him. He was a prey animal.

And unlike me, David had not, and would never, regain his morphing power.

Jake said that although there was no mission, Rachel wanted to see me. He said it was important. I said, <Okay.>

I flew to Rachel's house that night, after the

lights in her sisters' and mother's bedrooms were turned off. She had left the window open, as she often did. Sometimes I'd come by and do her homework for her. I don't know why. Some weird desire to stay in touch with my old life, I guess.

I flew silently, with the ease of long practice, through her open window and landed on her desk.

She was sitting in the dark with one of those little book lights on so she could read. She put down her book.

"Hi, Tobias," she whispered.

<Hi, Rachel. Listen, about the other day —>

"Something has happened," she interrupted.

<What?>

"Someone has come around asking about you."

My heart missed about a dozen beats. When it started again I had to gasp in air. <What do you mean, someone is asking about me?>

Rachel rolled off her bed. She was wearing a long sports jersey of some kind. It's what she wore to bed, I guess. I didn't recognize the team colors or the number. I was never very interested in sports, and now that whole thing means nothing at all to me.

She flicked on the dim lamp beside her bed and came over to me.

"Some lawyer. He says he was your father's

13

lawyer. And he's also representing some woman. She says her name is Aria. She says she's your cousin."

<Aria? Isn't that a song they sing in an opera?>

Rachel shrugged with that impatient, "What are you, an idiot? Pay attention!" way she has. "Who cares what her name means?"

<My cousin? Who does she say she's related to? I mean, who is her mother or father?>

"I didn't exactly cross-examine her," Rachel said snappishly.

I laughed. Don't ask me why, but Rachel being cranky always makes me laugh.

"This comes secondhand," Rachel clarified. "From Chapman."

That killed any amusement I was feeling. Chapman is the vice principal at my school. Or what used to be my school. He's also a high-ranking Controller. A human infested and utterly enslaved by the Yeerk in his head.

<Chapman?> I asked sharply. <How did he figure it out? Did he ask you specifically?>

She shook her head, a movement that caused her long, blond hair to shiver across her shoulders. "No. He was asking his daughter Melissa if she knew anything about Tobias. I just happened to be there."

<I don't trust it.>

"No one trusts anything about this," Rachel said. "Marco is in full-blown psycho paranoia mode. But for what it's worth, it sounded real to me. I mean, maybe Chapman knows more than he's letting his daughter know, but I didn't get the feeling he was interested in me."

<This still reeks. Marco's right to be paranoid. This smells bad.>

Rachel laughed. "Definitely. Chapman was all like, 'Tobias hasn't been in school in months. I contacted his last address and his guardian says he thought he was with some other aunt.'"

<Yeah, well, that's my family, all right,> I said, trying to sound lighthearted. Both of my parents are probably dead. I used to be sort of passed back and forth between an uncle and an aunt. One was a drunk and the other just couldn't be bothered.

No one wanted me. I don't say that to get pity; it's just reality. I couldn't blame them, I guess. I mean, they didn't ask to have a kid all of a sudden. And when I disappeared I don't guess either of them spent much time looking for me.

"Look, I know where this lawyer is staying," Rachel said. "Jake says we are all available to help check this out."

<Has to be a trap,> I said. <My father's

lawyer? Doesn't make any sense. When my mom disappeared and my dad died there wasn't any will or anything.>

"I don't know what to tell you," Rachel said.

<My father's lawyer. And some woman named Aria who is supposedly my cousin. It's a trap. Someone has figured out who I am.>

Rachel nodded, but not like she completely agreed. "Maybe. Probably. But I guess this woman has been in Africa all this time. She just got back and found out that no one knew where you were. I guess she contacted this lawyer of your dad's. She told him and Chapman she wanted to take you in."

<Take me in?>

"Give you a home, Tobias. A home."

CHAPTER 4

The lawyer's name was DeGroot. His office didn't look like much. It was in one of those strip malls with a convenience store at one end and a State Farm Insurance office on the other end.

It didn't look like a place to lay a trap. But that's the thing about traps: If they *looked* like traps, they wouldn't be very effective.

And the place did have one big problem for us: There was nowhere to hide any big morphs. Nowhere to conceal Jake's tiger or Rachel's grizzly bear.

Behind the building was a fenced-in Dumpster. Between the Dumpster and the back wall of the building was a narrow space. Dark enough, private enough for me to morph.

17

But I hesitated, floating above the building on the wonderful updrafts created by sun and concrete. I could see in the front window of the lawyer's office. I saw a secretary sitting at a desk. I saw some old magazines on tables in the waiting room. I couldn't see DeGroot.

Didn't matter. Seeing a man's face doesn't tell you much. Not when the most important thing about him is the slug hiding, wrapped around his brain.

I looked around. I saw some of the others. Jake and Cassie were sitting on the outside benches of a Taco Bell across the street. Jake was eating nachos, looking past Cassie at me. He knew I could see him. I did a little roll, you know, rocking side to side to say "hi." He raised a nacho to me, like he was making a toast.

I saw Marco coming out of the convenience store with a drink I could have taken a bath in. He acted like he'd just noticed Ax — in human morph, of course — and ambled over to say hello.

I could not see Rachel. But I knew she was in the Laundromat next door to the lawyer's office. She was my first backup. If I yelled for help she'd head into the Laundromat's bathroom, morph to grizzly bear, and come straight through the wall to save me.

I pitied any poor soul who happened to be using the bathroom if Rachel needed it.

Everyone in place. Everything was ready.

Still I hesitated. Not because the situation worried me. Not because I was afraid. It's very comforting, knowing you have an on-call grizzly bear.

Mostly I was just nervous. What was I going to discover? What was I going to learn? What temptations would I have to face?

Strange word, temptations. Strange concept. But that's what worried me most. Temptation.

Okay, Tobias, I told myself, *everyone can see you're dawdling. Get it over with.*

I swooped low over the roof of the strip mall and dropped swiftly down into the space behind the Dumpster. A lovely place: beer cans, weathered Dorito bags, candy wrappers, cigarette butts.

I landed on damp dirt and scraggly grass. And I began to morph.

It's funny, you know, because when Jake or one of the others becomes human, that's demorphing. But for me, the human is just another animal shape I can take on. Human DNA flows in my veins. My own human DNA, thanks to some neat work by the vastly powerful creature called the Ellimist.

On one of our first missions, I was trapped in the hawk body I now thought of as my own. Some months later the Ellimist used me to help some free Hork-Bajir escape. The Ellimist paid me for my services. But as usual with that unfathomable creature, there was a complication.

I had asked him to give me what I wanted most. I had assumed he'd make me human again. Instead, he left me a hawk but gave me back my morphing powers. And by twisting time itself, he brought me face-to-face with my old self and let me acquire my "own" DNA.

I could be my old human self. I could be that human boy for two hours and keep my morphing powers. Or I could remain more than two hours, be my old self forever, and forever lose my morphing ability.

Ax's people, the Andalites, know a little about the race or the individual called "Ellimist." No one knows for sure whether there's just one, or many, or whether it matters.

Anyway, the Andalites tell fairy stories of the Ellimists. They see them as tricksters. Unreliable. Creatures who use their power in unpredictable ways.

Well, the Ellimist had tricked me. He left me hanging, stuck between two impossible choices: become human and stop being an Animorph. Or live the life I live now.

All this flashed through my thoughts as I began to focus on the change I wanted to make. I felt the resentment I'd often felt for the Ellimist. But more, I felt my own indecision.

Slowly at first, because my mind was confused, then faster as I focused, my body began to change.

I grew taller. My sharp talons dulled, became pink and chubby toes. My leathery legs sprouted out of their feather sheath and thickened. I heard the bones stretching, becoming more solid.

I felt, as though it were happening far off, my internal organs shift and change. It was a squirmy, almost nauseating feeling. Which wasn't bad, considering the bizarre transformation that was going on in my insides.

My wing bones thickened and became heavy. Fingers began to emerge from the feathers, and at the same time, all over my body the feathers curled and twisted and disappeared.

In their place was pink skin and the minimal clothing I'd managed to incorporate in my morph.

My beak became soft, gradually melting into lips. Teeth appeared in my mouth with a grinding, disturbing sound that resonated in my expanding skull.

My hearing grew confused. My eyesight dimmed. It was as if anything more than a couple

21

of dozen feet away grew irrelevant. My eyes would not naturally focus on faraway things, preferring to see up close.

I felt exposed without my feathers. I felt deaf and blind. It was as if someone had gotten hold of the "brightness" and the "contrast" knobs on an old TV and turned them both down by half, then lowered the volume to a whisper.

Human senses work okay for what humans do. But compared to a hawk, a human is deaf, blind, and helpless.

Worst of all was the leaden pull of gravity. Not that a hawk ignores gravity. It's just not so . . . *final* when you have wings. I felt like someone had remade me in iron and the earth was one big magnet.

We'd left a paper bag with more appropriate clothing behind the Dumpster. I put it on as quickly as I could with unfamiliar fingers. Still, even clumsy fingers are a marvel. If there's one big physical advantage a human has over a hawk, it's the hand.

Yes, human brains are the best around. But the brain would be nothing without that hand.

I checked my clothing. I looked down at my shoes. I ran my tongue around inside my mouth, feeling the barbaric sensation of big, bony teeth.

"Hello," I said, trying out my voice. "Hi. Hi. My name is Tobias."

CHAPTER 5

"Hello. My name is Tobias. I . . ."

I hesitated. The secretary was looking at me skeptically. Like maybe I'd come in looking to borrow a quarter for the video game at the convenience store.

"My name is Tobias." I told her my last name. Weird. I could barely remember it. It felt like I was using an alias. "I think Mr. DeGroot wanted to talk to me."

She was puzzled. I looked at her nameplate. Ingrid.

"It's pronounced DeGroot. It rhymes with boat."

"Oh."

"Let me just check with Mr. DeGroot." She picked up her phone and punched a line. "Mr. DeGroot, there's a young boy named Tobias _____ out here. He says — Oh. All right."

She hung up the phone.

"I guess he does want to see you," she admitted. "Right through that door."

I checked the door. Fine. The lawyer's office was still sharing a wall with the Laundromat. If I started yelling it would take Rachel about three minutes to morph and come through that wall.

Three minutes is a very long time when you can't even fly.

I used the doorknob. Yes, human hands were very cool. As a bird I'd have been totally defeated by the doorknob.

DeGroot was younger than I'd expected. More in his twenties or thirties than really old. He was wearing a white shirt and red suspenders. His jacket was thrown casually over a chair.

He jumped up and smiled.

"So, *you* are Tobias."

"Yes. I'm Tobias."

He looked me up and down. I did the same to him.

"I've been hoping I could locate you, Tobias. Have a seat, please. Would you like some water? A soda? Coffee? No, I guess you don't drink coffee at your age. A soda? We have Coke, Diet

Coke. And we might have some Dr. Brown's cream soda. I'd have to have Ingrid check."

If he was getting ready to pull a gun and shoot me, or expecting to have Visser Three come storming in the door, he hid it very well.

I relaxed a little. But I was baffled. Water? Coffee? Soda? What was the right answer?

"Um . . . um . . ."

Good grief. You'd think it was Final Jeopardy and the category was Obscure Modern Poets. I was so out of practice being human.

"I'd like a Coke!" I practically yelled.

DeGroot pressed his intercom. "Ingrid, our young friend would like —"

"— a Coke. Yes, I heard him. All the way out here."

The lawyer and I stared at each other till the Coke came. I gripped the can self-consciously and pressed it to my beak. Lips.

It had been a long time since I'd tasted sugar. I almost burst out laughing. It was like being Ax in human morph. The taste of sugar was overwhelming! And the coldness. I hadn't felt cold in my mouth in a very long time.

"Tobias, where have you been staying? Your legal guardians both seemed to think the other one had you."

Not a question I wanted to answer. "I take care of myself."

DeGroot smiled. "No doubt. But you are underage. You can't 'take care of yourself.' Not legally."

"You can't lock me up," I said. Literally true. One thing about being an Animorph: No home, no building, no school, no jail or prison could hold me.

The lawyer looked pained. "That's not what I am talking about."

"Okay. What are you talking about?"

That seemed to set him back a little. It was weird. I had a toughness I'd never had when I was human. As a human I'd been a bully-magnet.

"Here's the thing. I represent your father's estate."

"My father is dead."

"Tobias . . ." He leaned across his desk. "Your father, that father, the man who died? That may not have been your *real* father."

"What?"

"I have a document . . . it's a strange situation. Very strange. Look, Tobias, I'm going to level with you. My father used to run this office. He's dead, too. He left this document along with the rest of his clients' papers. But on this he wrote me specific instructions. Very specific. On the date of your next birthday your father's last statement was to be read to you, if at all humanly possible."

I didn't know what to say. If this was a trap, it was a weird one.

"Are you okay? You don't seem surprised."

No, I didn't, I realized with a start. I had forgotten to make facial expressions. It was something I didn't do as a hawk.

"I am surprised," I said. I twisted my face into what I hoped was an expression of surprise. But it occurred to me that I was facing a new problem: He'd said he'd read the document on my next birthday.

When was my birthday? I couldn't exactly ask him.

"Now there's this new complication. A woman named Aria, who says she is your cousin. Your great-aunt's daughter. Apparently she's only just learned of your situation. She's a very acclaimed nature photographer and she's been on a long-term assignment in Africa. She wants to meet you."

"Why?"

"You're family. She wants to help you."

"Oh."

"She'd like to meet you tomorrow. At the hotel where she's staying. If that's okay. It's the Hyatt downtown. Do you know where that is?"

I could have said, yes, I am familiar with their roof. A peregrine falcon has a nest there in a niche in the radio tower. And the thermals are

great, sweeping up the south face of the building, warm air radiating up from the street below
and gaining strength from the sunlight reflected
off all those windows.

What I did say was, "Yeah, I know where it
is."

"She's very concerned for you."

"Uh-huh."

"Do you need money? A place to spend the
night?"

"No, I'm fine."

He shrugged doubtfully. "You look healthy
enough. Well dressed."

I almost laughed. Rachel had picked out my
wardrobe. I looked like a poster boy for Tommy
Hilfiger.

"I get by okay. Um . . . so when did you say
you're going to read this document?"

"On your birthday."

"Ah. Okay. Bye."

CHAPTER 6

My birthday. When was my birthday? This month?

What month were we in?

I left the office and walked to the convenience store. Ax and Marco studiously avoided noticing me. Ax's human morph face was smeared with something I could only hope was chocolate.

I didn't even look at them. No nod, no wink, nothing. If we were being followed the slightest thing would give us away.

The signal for "danger" was me going to the donut display and looking inside. The signal for "okay" was me picking up a Mounds bar and putting it back down.

I toyed with the Mounds bar. The guy at the counter said, "You gonna buy that?"

Ax and Marco left. I went to the newspaper rack. I checked the date. The month. Yes, that was my birth month. Today was the twenty-second.

My birthday was . . . the twenty-fifth! Yes. That was it. Probably.

I waited till Marco and Ax were clear then I went outside. I blinked at the sun and almost flapped my wings.

My father! My father was not my father? There was some "real" father somewhere? Also dead or gone?

That was a lot of coincidence. And some long-lost cousin showing up within days of when this "father's" will was supposed to be read to me?

Way too much coincidence.

I started walking. I was heading to the nearby park to demorph at a spot we'd chosen in advance.

Halfway there, I heard Jake's thought-speak voice in my head. <I think you're being followed. A big guy in a suit.>

I didn't wonder too much where Jake was. In the sky somewhere. Up flying free.

We had planned for this. I glanced across the street and saw a Speedy Muffler King and an Applebee's. I headed for the Applebee's.

Across traffic. Trotting, like I'd suddenly realized I was hungry.

<Yep. He's following you,> Jake reported.

In the front door of Applebee's. Fast, fast toward the men's room before my tail could catch sight of me again.

Then a quick cut left, past the bathroom, into the kitchen.

Waiters and waitresses were running around, pushing, laughing, yelling. The cooks were banging pots. I pushed past the dishwasher, looking for the back door.

"Hey, if you're looking for the bathroom . . ." someone called out as I blew past.

Out the back door. I broke into a run. There was a residential street of small homes behind the restaurant. Down a connecting alley, I cut right again, heading once more for the park.

I wasn't too worried. Someone might think he could follow me without being noticed. But I had eyes in the sky watching over me.

<You lost him,> Jake reported.

I trotted on toward the park. They had a covered but open kind of rest room thing. You know, with a roof, only the walls didn't go all the way up?

I found an empty stall and waited.

<Tobias, you're clear,> Cassie said.

I demorphed. Back to hawk. I flew up and out

of the stall, up away from humans and back into the blue sky.

Only then did it hit me full force: Someone wanted me. Family. Wanted to take care of me.

Unless, of course, what they really wanted was to learn my secrets.

And then kill me.

CHAPTER 7

I should have met with the others. That was the plan. But once I was back in the sky, I just didn't want to.

I didn't want to have to sit down and explain it all to them. I guess, too, I didn't want to have to deal with Cassie's hopefulness and Rachel's concern and Marco's abrasive skepticism.

I didn't want it all analyzed and picked apart. I knew the routine. Cassie would make me go over everything, word by word, gesture by gesture, expression by expression. Cassie has an amazing talent for understanding other people and their motives. She would want to understand all she could about DeGroot.

Marco would be different. He would barely listen before he started zeroing in on all the problems and inconsistencies.

Rachel would pace restlessly, angrily, looking for some way to make me safe. Looking for some action to take. Jake would wait and listen calmly, and judge.

I didn't want my friends thinking for me. I didn't want them to decide what I felt. I wanted to do it alone.

This was mine. My problem. My hope. My choice.

I flew. Flew and flew, circling higher and higher on lush thermals that felt as if they could lift me effortlessly beyond the clouds.

Below and behind, I saw a falcon I knew as Jake. And a harrier I knew as Cassie. They saw me. Jake, at least, could easily have caught up with me. But they let me go. I guess they knew I needed to think.

I circled up till I could feel the ceiling of a flat-bottomed cumulus cloud right above me. Then I translated my altitude into distance and headed for the woods. Headed for a very specific place in the woods, far back, far from any trail.

I had been to this place twice before. Once when the Ellimist showed us all the way. Once when I went there only to hear an amazing story. But even now, even knowing precisely where it was, even with all my hawk vision focused, all my innate direction-finding ability carefully attuned, I had a hard time finding it.

Call it a spell. That's what the Ellimist had done: He had cast a fairy-tale spell over this place, making it almost impossible for any mere mortal to find it. The eyes slid away. The feathers did not feel a breeze that blew from it. The ears heard no sound that came from it.

It was the valley of the Hork-Bajir. The *free* Hork-Bajir.

Jara Hamee and Ket Halpak had been the couple who'd escaped their Yeerk slave masters. How much the Ellimist had intervened . . . well, he would say he never intervenes in the affairs of other species. But Jara and Ket had evaded their Yeerks and avoided recapture with help from us. And they had come to this concealed valley.

Since then, others had come. Some were escapees. Others had been born into freedom.

That's where I flew. To the valley of the Hork-Bajir.

The last time I'd come, they'd been surprised. This time was different. This time, as I flew through the narrow opening of the valley, I saw two dozen Hork-Bajir standing, looking up at the sky, waiting.

When they saw me they began to point and wave. I thought I recognized Jara and Ket. Standing at their center was the young Hork-Bajir girl named Toby. Named after me. She was Jara and Ket's child. And she was what the Hork-Bajir call a "seer."

The Hork-Bajir are not the geniuses of the galaxy. They may look like death and destruction on two legs, but the blades that adorn their seven-foot-tall bodies are designed for stripping edible bark from trees.

That is not what their slave master Yeerks use them for. The Hork-Bajir have been made into the shock troops of the Yeerk Empire.

In any case, whether fearsome or sweet, the Hork-Bajir are not an intellectual species. Except for the very rare genetic anomalies they call "seers."

Looking down at the gaggle of waiting Hork-Bajir, I easily spotted Toby. I'd have spotted her even without knowing her. The rest of the group had the dopey, dim expressions of Teletubbies. Toby had the kind of eyes that looked through you and made you feel like you needed to pull a robe on over your brain.

"Tobias!" Jara Hamee yelled happily. "Friend Tobias! Friend."

<Hi, Jara. Hi, Ket. Hello, Toby.>

"Toby say you come," Ket said, nodding with great satisfaction. "Toby say, 'Tobias will come.'"

"Yes," Jara agreed. "Toby say, 'Friend Tobias will come.'"

"You are here," Ket said.

Like I said, the Hork-Bajir are long on decent and kind and sweet and generous, and a bit short on witty, clever, and brilliant. If Marco spent a day with the Hork-Bajir, he'd lose his mind and run screaming away looking for someone, anyone, who'd get a joke.

I landed on a nice, level branch just a foot above their weird, forward-raked head blades. <Why did you expect me?>

"We need you, Tobias," Toby said.

I sighed inwardly. I didn't want to be needed. I wanted some peace and quiet and a chance to think.

But that feeling evaporated the instant Toby explained.

"One of the children, a male named Bek, is missing. He has left the valley. We fear that he may be taken by humans or by human-Controllers. That he may be harmed. Killed. Or worse, made into a Controller."

CHAPTER 8

Once before when I was feeling low, I went to the Hork-Bajir valley. They'd made me feel better. After all, the Hork-Bajir think I'm their liberator. They think I'm George Washington or whatever. It's hard not to feel good under those circumstances.

But obviously, this visit was going to be different.

<You searched the entire valley?> I demanded.

"Yes. Search," Jara said. "Look and look and look."

"Cry, 'Bek, Bek!'" another Hork-Bajir added helpfully.

"Bek, Bek!" Ket confirmed.

"Bek is not in the valley," Toby said. "I . . . we found tracks leading out of the valley. The right size for a Hork-Bajir of his age."

I said several words I can't repeat. Jara Hamee asked what they meant. <Never mind,> I said. I couldn't believe this. A Hork-Bajir child missing! Wandering the woods alone. Or worse: not alone.

<How long has he been gone?>

"Since this time yesterday," the young seer said.

<Oh, man. I have to get back to the others. We'll start a search. But I don't think our chances are very good.> Suddenly a thought occurred to me. <Do you think Bek could lead people back here? Would he be able to find his way back? The Ellimist has laid some kind of weird spell on this place.>

Toby looked wary. "No, Bek would not know the way back. But we are able to find our way back."

That made me stare. <What do you mean? You leave the valley?>

"Yes, Tobias. How else can we free our brothers and sisters?" She waved an encompassing arm around the group. "How else have these Hork-Bajir come to freedom?"

<I . . . I guess I just assumed the Ellimist made it happen.>

Toby grinned the frightening Hork-Bajir grin. "We make it happen. We go at night and raid places where we know Hork-Bajir are."

<The Yeerk pool?> I asked incredulously.

Toby looked down. "Tobias, we owe you a great deal."

"Freedom," Ket Halpak said solemnly. "Hork-Bajir free. Tobias make free."

<But?> I said a little sarcastically.

"But . . . but the place where we liberate Hork-Bajir is a secret Yeerk facility that is being built. Not in your city. In the human town beyond the far end of this valley. Tobias . . . it is very important for us to continue freeing our brothers and sisters. We are few. We must become many. To fight the Yeerks. Also . . ." She let it hang there.

<Un. Be. Lievable,> I said. <You "seers" really are a different breed, aren't you?> I said harshly. <You're looking for the day when the Yeerks leave, aren't you? You need enough numbers so that humans don't just slap you all in a zoo.>

Toby looked proud. "The Hork-Bajir trusted Andalites to save us from the Yeerks. The Andalites failed. The Andalites took care of their own. We must do the same. We are grateful to the humans called Animorphs. But do you say we should trust all humans?"

Well, she had me there. It was way too easy to see a day when the Yeerks were defeated and these Hork-Bajir were left behind on Earth. What would happen to them? Humans didn't exactly have an unblemished record of tolerance for different races. After all, before this valley had belonged to the Hork-Bajir, it had probably been inhabited by Native Americans.

<You're worried that if I know about this secret Yeerk construction project my friends and I will attack it?>

"Yes."

<Do you think Bek may have gone there?>

"We don't know. He may have followed the scent trails left by our raiders." She sounded doubtful. "It is possible. But he did not leave from that end of the valley."

<Ah. Swell. Perfect. You know, I came up here looking for a break from life.>

The seer smiled. "If you promise not to destroy the place, I will show you how to find it."

I sighed. <I have to talk to Jake and the others. Jake's going to want to go after this facility.>

Toby started to say something, but I interrupted her. <You have my word we won't do anything unless you approve. I'll deal with Jake. In the meantime, we'll start searching elsewhere. But be ready in case I come back. Because if I come back, it will mean I need you.>

41

It was Jara who stepped forward then. Toby may have been the brains, but Jara and Ket were the heart of this tiny community. Jara put his big, dangerous claw out, palm up, and I hopped into it. He lifted me up to his goblin face and said, "Tobias ask the Hork-Bajir. Hork-Bajir give. Always. Forever. Anything. Even life. Jara Hamee never forget."

Toby nodded her agreement.

Well, what are you going to do? People like that you pretty much have to try and save.

CHAPTER 9

Morning. The meadow.

My meadow.

I saw the other hawk. He was flying, inscribing low circles over the meadow. His eyes were aimed downward, looking for breakfast. But he saw me.

I knew he saw me, because if our roles were reversed, I would see him.

He was wondering why . . . no, that was wrong. He wasn't wondering. He was a true red-tailed hawk. Hawks don't wonder. The question "why" is owned entirely by humans. At least, on Earth it is. Only Homo sapiens asks why. *Buteo jamaicensis* — red-tailed hawks — don't ask at all.

He saw me. He knew I was a threat. He watched. He waited. He expected my attack. When my attack came, he would fight. If my attack did not come, he would come after me. It would be a "show" fight. Bluff and threaten and see who ran first. But it could also end up being a very real fight.

I saw him drop down swiftly on some target. A few seconds later he flapped his way back up into view. His talons were empty. He'd missed.

Not enough prey in the meadow. Not enough for both of us. One of us had to go. Or both of us would starve.

I sat on my perch and saw the twitch of grass that told me a rabbit was coming out of its hole. We all have to eat. Rabbits, too.

My opponent was too far away and at the wrong angle to see what I saw. I opened my wings and swooped out of the shadows.

This time I would take one of the rabbits. This time my talons would close on squirming, living flesh.

This time the rabbit would die so that I could live.

I saw them! Yes! The mother and one of the babies. Just my size, the perfect prey. Slow moving, unaware, unlike the wily mother.

I was approaching them on a perfect glide path. I was in the mother rabbit's blind spot. I opened my talons wide and moved them forward. I trimmed my wings and tail just so. Just perfectly to intercept the little rabbit on its next heedless hop.

Now! Now! Now! Drop and strike!

<Aaaahhhh!>

The vision seized my mind again. I was the rabbit, not the hawk!

I saw the talons! Too late! I tried to hop away but the panic froze me in place. I shook with terror. I could see death coming from the sky, but I could not move.

<Noooooo!> I screamed and broke off. <Noooooo!>

I flapped up and away, and the awful vision faded. The baby rabbit hopped to his mother's side.

<What is happening to me?!> I yelled to an empty sky. <What is happening to me?>

CHAPTER 10

"Just tell me this," Marco raged. "When do we get a vacation? I mean, Ben-Hur rowing that Roman galley while the guy whipped him and the other guy banged on that big drum got more downtime than we do."

We were in Cassie's barn. It was the next day, after the others got back from school. I was in the rafters, in my usual place. From there I could look out through the hayloft to see Cassie's house and the driveway. And I could listen to sounds coming from outside. I could know whether anyone was sneaking up on us.

"Our lives have become Nintendo games," Marco went on, enjoying the sound of his own outrage. "We're always walking down some dark hallway with our blasters drawn and there's an endless array of enemy guys. We blow 'em up, but they keep coming. When do we get to hit the pause button? When do we get to switch over to a nice, peaceful Riven? When do we get to turn off the power and put down the joystick and just veg out with some HBO? When do —"

"When do we get to shut you up?" Rachel interrupted. "When do we get to switch *you* off? I mean, good grief, Marco, you act like you have something better to do. Before we became Animorphs your entire day consisted of figuring out which girl to annoy next."

Marco grinned. "And now I always know which girl to annoy next." He put his arm around Rachel and laid his head on her shoulder.

She laughed and shoved him away.

It was just a dumb little routine, but I felt a flash of jealousy. There are little intimacies that most humans can have that I can't. I can't shake hands or hug or lay my head on anyone's shoulder.

And, as I'd expected, Cassie had questioned me closely, listening intently to everything I related about my meeting with DeGroot. Marco came up with about eight different ways it could all be a scam.

But then I'd told them all this new piece of information: A Hork-Bajir kid was on the loose.

That's when Marco had started ranting and raving.

"Okay," Jake said, "we have a lot happening
at once. And we can't blow off any of it. We need
to find out if DeGroot is for real or a Controller.
We need to find out the same about this possible
cousin Aria. And we need to try and find this little, lost Hork-Bajir. Twenty-four hours plus last
night, plus this morning while we were in school.
Coming up on forty-eight hours he's been missing."

"I hate to think of what could be happening
to him," Cassie said.

Jake nodded. But Marco said, "No, wait. You
should try and think of what's happening to him.
What are the possibilities?"

<I assume that any human would recognize
this Hork-Bajir child as an alien,> Ax wondered.

"No. Not necessarily," Cassie said.

"Most people don't believe you aliens exist,"
Rachel said.

Ax nodded, a gesture he'd picked up from humans. <Then what *might* a human think this
creature is?>

"Deformed," Cassie speculated. "Affected by
birth defects. Or seriously sick."

<The average, fairly decent human would
think of taking it to a hospital,> I said.

"Or calling an ambulance," Cassie added.

<The average not-so-decent human might decide to shoot it,> I said. <Or stick it in a cage and charge people to look at the freak.>

Jake nodded agreement. "Yeah. Okay. Marco? Get on the Internet and look for any news reports or whatever. Ax? You help him. Cassie and I will go back to the valley entrance, morph wolves, and see if we can pick up Bek's scent. Rachel, you're with Tobias. Figure out if DeGroot and this Aria woman are Controllers. Follow them. Watch them. How long do we have till your birthday, Tobias?"

<Um . . . three days?> I asked.

"Today's the twenty-third. When's your birthday?"

<The twenty-fifth. I think. Twenty-sixth?>

Marco laughed, then I guess he realized I wasn't kidding.

<I don't . . . I don't exactly remember. Not for sure. But I think it's in three days.> I forced a laugh. <Just don't ask me how old I am in bird years.>

CHAPTER 11

I felt uncomfortable being paired with Rachel. She'd seen me eating roadkill. She hadn't mentioned it, and I didn't think she would. Rachel's blunt but sensitive enough, too.

Still, uncomfortable or not, I wasn't going to start arguing with Jake. I have my problems in life. He has his. I'm not going to complicate his situation.

Besides, what could I say? I'd rather work with Cassie because she doesn't know I eat roadkill?

Rachel went into her bald eagle morph. I've seen her do it many times before, of course, but for some reason this time it fascinated me. Is that the right word? No, it mesmerized me.

Rachel is a beautiful girl. She's beautiful in that way you know will last her whole life. She'll be a beautiful woman. But beauty alone isn't that big a thing. What makes Rachel "Rachel" is what's inside.

And watching her morph to eagle was like seeing her soul emerge through her flesh.

Feather patterns appeared across her skin. The golden hair gave way to the characteristic white feathers of the baldie's crown. Her arm bones narrowed and hollowed and grew feathers to become wings.

Her face, never exactly soft or inviting, became forbidding and intense. Her blue eyes turned golden brown and glared with the fierce glare of a raptor. Her lips became the eagle's huge beak.

She grew smaller. But she was becoming one of the largest birds in existence.

Was she more beautiful to me because she was a bird now? No, of course not. For one thing, eagles and hawks don't mate. For another, her eagle morph is male.

But sometimes it seemed to me that this body suited her better than her own. Her own body misled people with superficial resemblances to the glossy images of magazine models. This body was Rachel: fast, strong, smart, intense, and dangerous.

<Ready?> she asked.

<Ready,> I said.

She spread her wings. So much broader than my own. I am proud of being a red-tailed hawk, but there is no avoiding the fact that the human eye is drawn to a bald eagle. People can see me and think, *What is that, a big brown crow?* But when you see a baldie floating on the air, with its six-foot wingspread and yellow beak and unmistakable white head, you know you're looking at something special.

I read once that Benjamin Franklin wanted the wild turkey to be the official symbol of the United States. But come on. He must never have seen a bald eagle.

We caught a late afternoon thermal and rode it high into the air. Rachel had her wings, but I had my experience, so I kept pace with her easily enough. Not to brag, but when you can add human intelligence onto bird instinct, you get so you can outfly just about anything in the air. Instinct only takes you so far.

<I didn't mention it to Jake, but I've already spent the morning observing DeGroot,> I said.

<Why him? Why not this Aria person?> Rachel asked.

<I know him. He was easy to observe. Plus . . . >

<Plus what?>

I'd been about to say that the very idea of Aria made me nervous. Unsettled. <Nothing. Let's go see if we can find her. I know what hotel she's in. I know the room. I morphed to human and called the hotel.>

<How did you get a quarter for the phone?>

<With these eyes? Coins shine in the sunlight. You fly around outside coin-op Laundromats or the drive-through lane at a McDonald's, you'll find a dropped quarter sooner or later.>

Rachel laughed like that was the funniest thing in the world. <You are the world champion of coping with weird situations,> she said.

<Yeah, well, not always. Sometimes I just wimp out.>

<What do you mean?>

<Let's crank it to the west a little more, catch this trailing breeze, and take a load off our wings,> I said.

<Ah. Something you don't want to talk about. That's cool.>

We turned west and felt the propulsion of the wind coming around behind us. Flying is a lot like sailing. You can fly against the wind, but it'll wear you down fast. You can sort of tack, flying against the wind by turning at angles to it. But when the wind is cooperating and going your way, hey, you ride it and be thankful.

<It's no big thing,> I said with a dismissive laugh. <A little bird-on-bird problem.>

<So give me the four-one-one, already,> she grumped. <We have ten, twenty minutes of flying and I forgot to bring a book to read.>

<It's nothing. It's this hawk that's trying to move in on my meadow.>

I felt like an idiot the minute the words were out of my head. This was like the "old" Tobias style: treating people to displays of stupidity and weakness. No wonder I'd gotten beat up so often when I was human. It was like I was begging people to sneer at me.

<Brilliant, Tobias,> I muttered to myself. <Rachel, of all people is really going to appreciate some pathetic story of how you can't stand up to a bird.>

<What, is he bigger than you?>

Why didn't I just keep my mouth shut? <Forget it. I just haven't decided the right time to kick his butt.>

Yeah, right. That was believable.

<There's the hotel. We need the twenty-third floor,> I said. <Room twenty-three-oh-six. It's supposed to be facing the city view.>

CHAPTER 12

My heart was beating even faster than usual. I might be about to see a cousin who wanted to take me in. Or I might be sniffing around the edges of a clever trap.

I counted up the floors to twenty-three. We swept around the building to the city side. It is especially thrilling flying around tall buildings. Something about being *outside* a skyscraper really reminds the human part of you how high up you are. You can imagine humans suddenly *outside* and picture their helpless terror as they fall, and . . . well, like I said, it reminds you.

<With the sun at this angle I'm having a hard time seeing inside the windows,> I complained.

<Really? Not me,> Rachel said.

<Bald eagles hunt fish,> I pointed out. <Your eyes are evolved to see down through water, even if there are reflections on the water. I eat mice and rabbits.>

<Rabbits?>

<You take what you can get. And don't start in with Thumper from *Bambi*, or Peter Rabbit, or the Easter Bunny. Rabbits are prey, just like mice.>

<I was just gonna say they sounded tastier than mice. I mean, people eat rabbits. Or at least they used to. In the old cowboy movies didn't they shoot rabbits and cook 'em up with a mess o' beans?>

<Absolutely. Exactly. Nothing wrong with eating a rabbit.>

<Unless he's named "Bugs." Hey, I see a woman in that room. Um . . . third window from the end.>

<I can't see clearly.>

<Probably a good thing. She's changing.>

<Ah. You mean she's changing clothes, right? Not morphing.>

<She's morphing from a pair of sweatpants and T-shirt into a dress. The dress is, oh, about three, four years out of date.>

<So maybe she really was in Africa. If that's even her.>

<Or maybe she doesn't keep up with fashion.

I see a lot of camera equipment. That'd fit with the whole nature photographer thing.>

<The glare is shifting. Is it safe for me to look?>

<Are you always this nice about being a Peeping Tom?>

<I am never a Peeping Tom,> I said sharply. Then I softened my tone. <I cannot use my superpowers for evil.>

Rachel laughed. <Okay to look now.>

I banked into a turn, flapped to keep my altitude, then glided as slowly as I could, forty feet out from the window.

She was maybe twenty-five or thirty. She had dark hair, pulled back into a ponytail. Not tall, not short. Thin. She seemed very tan.

<Does she look like anyone in your family?> Rachel asked.

<No. I mean, I don't know. According to DeGroot I have some father I didn't even know about. So who knows if she looks like family?>

<How do we find out?>

I didn't answer. The truth is, I hadn't really heard Rachel. I was off in my own mind, watching the strange woman who said she wanted to take care of me.

Why? Why would someone want to take care of me? She didn't know me. So why? Because of some vague family loyalty thing? Maybe. I guess some families are like that. You know, they feel connected to anyone who shares a biological connection to them. But my family wasn't that way. Not the ones I'd met, anyway.

My mother disappeared and my father died when I was little. I barely remembered either of them. I had pictures, of course. Back when I was human. But now when I tried to remember them I couldn't tell whether the memories were real or just something I'd made up.

Sometimes I wondered if it was all an illusion. That I'd never had a mother and father. That I'd never really been human.

I was a freak of nature. No, that wasn't right, either. Nature at its most perverse could not create me. I was a freak of technology. Of alien technology.

I was a bird with the mind of a human boy. Or I was a boy with the body of a bird. Either way, that woman I saw through the glass, the woman now channel-surfing with her remote control and stopping at CNN, that woman did not know me.

Not the old me or the real me.

Surprise, Cousin Aria, your adopted son is a red-tailed hawk.

<I say, ahem, how do we find out?> Rachel asked.

<What? Oh. I guess we follow her. Watch her.

Observe. If she's a Controller she'll need to go to the Yeerk pool within the next three days.>

<We can't watch her continuously,> Rachel said.

<Maybe not,> I admitted. <But maybe we can find out enough. Look! She's getting a phone call.>

<She looks puzzled. Now she's . . . excited. There she goes!>

Aria . . . if this was Aria . . . hefted a camera bag onto her shoulder. She paused in front of a full-length mirror, adjusting her hair and checking her clothes carefully.

<Don't worry about your hair,> Rachel sniped, <do something about that dress.>

I laughed. But at the same time something bothered me about what I'd just seen. Something . . .

But then the woman was out the door of her room and out of sight.

<We should swing around to the front door. Watch her come out,> Rachel said.

<Yeah. Let's just hope she doesn't drive or catch a cab.>

<Why?>

<Ever tried flying fast enough to keep up with a car?>

CHAPTER 13

<Oh, man! She's going for a cab!> I yelled as the hotel doorman waved for a taxi.

<Traffic's pretty bad. Maybe we can stay with her,> Rachel said.

<Not by staying in the air, we can't,> I said grimly.

<You have a plan?>

<Rachel, I have a plan even you will think is insane,> I said. <See that cop car? Going the same general direction as the cab? See the lights on top?>

Rachel laughed. <Okay, that actually *is* insane. Let's do it!>

We dove, hurtling down out of the sky. What I had in mind wasn't exactly subtle. It was dangerous and would make heads turn as we raced through the city streets.

But it could possibly work.

The red lights atop the police car were mounted on a raised bar. There was a light at either end, and a couple of feet of open bar between.

The cab headed east down a major boulevard. So did the police car. They were only doing twenty miles an hour in the traffic, but hawks and eagles can't just fly long distances in a straight line. We need to turn, to ride the thermals upward. Even at twenty miles an hour the cab could lose us.

Down we swooped, turning height into speed.

Down, down, me slightly in front.

<Rachel, line up behind me, but watch the turbulence from my wings!>

She lined up behind me and we swept down from twenty-something floors up to just above street level, executing a smooth glide path that an airline pilot would have been proud of.

<Keep up your speed!>

<We're going faster than them, we'll overshoot!> Rachel cried.

<Are *you* telling *me* how to fly?>

<No, sir!> Rachel yelled in that giddy way she gets whenever she's an inch away from utter disaster. <Hah HAH!>

The cop car moved horizontally. We came down at an angle. The two lines would meet . . . now!

<Flare!> I swept my wings forward, killed just a hint of my airspeed, opened my talons, spread them wide, and . . . yes! Snagged the crossbar and held on.

Rachel grabbed with one talon but missed with the other. She folded her wings and the wind current slammed her back.

<Keep your profile!> I cried. <Open your wings. Surf, don't ride.>

Somehow she made sense of my gibbering. She lunged with her other talon and caught the bar. She muscled her body forward into a flying profile. She spread her massive wings.

And off we went. A red-tailed hawk and a bald eagle riding the roof of a cop car, wings open, beaks forward, talons straining to take the pressure.

<Now this doesn't look too strange!> Rachel laughed, still high from the rush of danger.

Drivers behind and beside us stared, mouths open. Some to the point where they barely avoided crashing into one another. But the police beneath us remained oblivious.

<Someone is going to yell to the cops that we're up here,> I worried.

<Nah,> Rachel reassured me. <No one goes

out of their way to attract a cop's attention while they're driving. We'll be saved by people's guilty consciences.>

One very odd-looking police car continued down the boulevard, shadowing the cab from a distance of three or four car lengths. We rode for two miles that way, till we'd reached the edge of the city, out where the buildings grew smaller, older, and shabbier. We were passing the airport. A big 747 roared by overhead.

And then . . .

<Ahhhh!>

Red lights swirled all around us. The car surged forward. Wind resistance doubled and I could barely hold on. Then came the siren.

Think police sirens are loud? Try having better-than-human hearing and being eight inches from the siren itself. Then add in four jet engines from a slow-moving jumbo jet.

<Aaaaahhhh! They got a call!>

The cop car took off. In a second we'd pass the cab. No! A sudden turn, and the cab and police car were separating at a rapid clip.

Too fast for us to keep our wings open. We were moving at fifty, maybe sixty miles an hour. We closed our wings and hunkered down as close to the bar as we could crouch. I tucked my head low and kept my tail feathers tightly closed.

Now we were just alongside the airport. Another jet, a smaller 737 this time, was readying for takeoff. But before it gathered speed, something much smaller rose from the tarmac.

A helicopter.

The helicopter lifted off and headed at right angles to us. It was going the same direction as the cab.

<I have another really bad idea,> I said.

<No.>

<I'm doing it!> I yelled.

<How do I do it?> Rachel screamed.

<Time it! Release. Just a little tail for lift, barely open your wings, use your head to turn!>

<When?>

<NOW!>

I released my grip. I opened my tail feathers and cocked them ever so slightly upward. So little wing that my wings might as well have been tail fins of a rocket.

And a good thing, too, because I *was* a rocket.

I blew through the air like a feather missile, catching just enough lift, turning with only a slight movement of my head . . .

I shot up beneath the helicopter, swerved to match its direction, rolled over on my back, opened my talons, and . . .

<Ooowwww!> I took the jolt as my talons closed around the strut of the landing skid.

Rachel was just behind me. She turned and opened her talons, but she hadn't prepared for the severe downdraft of wind from the helicopter's rotors.

A miss!

Rachel's talons missed their mark, and she wasn't going to get another shot.

<I'll see you later!> I yelled to her.

<Not much later,> she laughed. <Take a look. The cab pulled in down there.>

I had pulled off a completely impossible move. For absolutely no reason.

<It was still way cool,> Rachel said. But she laughed some more as I released my hard-won grip on the helicopter and floated in embarrassment toward the dirt field where the cab was now disgorging Aria.

CHAPTER 14

It took a moment for me to realize what I was looking at. It was a shabby-looking building from the air. But the truth is, most buildings look pretty bad from the air. You just see roofs and air conditioners.

The building itself was one story, but with a false facade that would have made it look much bigger to a person approaching from ground level. It was fronted by a dirt parking lot with a few cars. In the back was a dirty green lagoon — shallow water bordered by a rickety-looking wooden railing.

There were two alligators sunning themselves on the mud banks of this tiny lagoon.

The lot to the left of the building was a liquor

store. To the right of the main building, seemingly attached to it, was a miniature golf course. The theme was apparently "pirates." A plaster pirate ship served as a centerpiece.

<It's one of those crappy roadside zoo things,> Rachel reported, having swept low enough to see the garish signs clearly. <It's called "Frank's Safari Land and Putt-Putt Golf.">

<Catchy name,> I said.

<It's just a good thing Cassie isn't here. She hates these places. I mean, she *hates* these places. She'd have us go in there and free all the animals.>

<Maybe that's why Aria is here,> I suggested. <She's a nature photographer, after all. She must hate places like this, too.>

<Maybe,> Rachel said skeptically.

I banked a turn and went low to check out a sort of marquee that advertised to passing cars. It was one of those signs where they use big plastic letters.

The sign said ALL NEW! DEADLY MIDGET FREAK! THE LIVING RAZOR!

<Oh, man. We have trouble,> I said.

<Will it involve trying to snag onto a helicopter in midair?> Rachel asked with a laugh. <And by the way, it may have been unnecessary, but it was SO cool!>

<"The Living Razor,"> I said, quoting the sign. <"Deadly Midget Freak.">

<What's a living razor?> Rachel wondered.

<Don't know for sure, but I have a bad feeling about this. I think we need to get inside that building.>

<Well, we could demorph to human and walk right in. If we had money for a ticket.>

Demorph to human? Not me. I had to *morph* to human. I let it go.

<It's two bucks each,> I said.

<I have got to learn how to morph a credit card.>

<We could always sneak in as cockroaches,> I said. <I doubt a couple of roaches would even be noticed in that place. Let alone a couple of houseflies.>

<Oh man, I hate doing insects. You know —>

<Uh-oh. I feel a Rachel idea coming on.>

<Oh please, after your idea of riding a cop car then rocketing off to grab a helicopter? You're going to diss *my* idea?>

<Ooookay. Fair enough.>

<I was just noticing there's only one old man watching the front door. And I have to tell you, I don't think all his hair is exactly real.>

<What?>

<Head for the Putt-Putt pirate ship. We can demorph in there. I'll be right along.>

With that, Rachel swooped down from the sky on a glide path toward the old man, who was sitting on a stool just outside the door to Frank's Safari Land.

Talons open, she raked the man's head.

"Hey!" he yelled. "That's my hair!"

The big bald eagle flew slow and low, carrying what looked like a dead muskrat, but was in fact the man's toupee. The man took off after her. I headed for the big plaster pirate ship. A few moments later Rachel joined me, laughing as she demorphed.

<Okay, what did you do with the poor man's toupee?>

<Well, let's just say one of those alligators has a whole new look.>

We demorphed inside the dusty, cobwebbed interior of the fake ship and had to squeeze out through a tiny access door. No one stopped us. No one noticed then, or when we walked brazenly through the front door of Frank's Safari Land.

CHAPTER 15

Inside it was about what I'd expected. A very sad place. Miserable, unhappy animals in cages a tenth the size they should have been. Dim lighting that was swallowed up by the black-draped walls.

A mangy fox paced restlessly. A pair of lynx slept, crammed into a cage that would have been small for a house cat. There was an aged barn owl, an adolescent deer, a pair of sheep. There was a Shetland pony in a circular pen, saddle on its back, saddle sores plainly visible. A sign said PONY RIDES $2.50.

A small female black bear was in a cage so low she could not rear up to her full height.

Rachel leaned close to whisper in my ear. "I was going to say we shouldn't tell Cassie about this place, but you know what? Let's *do* tell her. She'll get Jake to go along with stomping this horrible place out of existence. What is the matter with people? I mean, I'm not exactly Ms. Tree-hugging-don't-eat-meat-let-animals-vote, but come on, this sucks. They want to treat a bear like that, I'll come back here and introduce these dirtbags to a *real* bear. See if 'Frank' can stick my grizzly in a little cage. I'll cage *him*!"

I smiled with my human lips. The thing is, I knew Rachel wasn't exaggerating. If Jake didn't stop her, the "Frank" of Frank's Safari was going to be getting a visit from a big, shaggy, very annoyed, seven-foot-tall grizzly bear.

Then we went around a dark corner into a small side room. There stood Aria and a man. I backed away quickly. But not so quickly that I failed to see the occupant of that small room.

There, in a raised cage with two spotlights intersecting on him, was a young Hork-Bajir.

He was only three feet tall, practically a newborn by Hork-Bajir standards. His blades were very sharp, like human baby teeth are, but small and not as rigid or dangerous as an adult's blades.

His tail was stubby, barely formed. The forehead blades were just bumps.

His clawed hands were wrapped around the bars of his cage. He was gazing with pathetic hope at Aria.

"Whoa," Rachel whispered.

"Yeah."

We glided back out of sight, not that either Aria or the man with her had noticed us.

"Look, lady, I'm not trying to bust your chops here. But if you want to take pictures, that's extra."

"But, Mr. Hallowell —"

"Call me Frank."

"Okay, Frank. I'm a professional nature photographer. I would be happy to give you some copies of the pictures in payment."

The man sneered. "I need a picture of the freak, I'll take a Polaroid. Uh-uh. This little monster is going to make me some cash. I've already contacted a newspaper. They're sending a guy out. He decides this is a good freak, he'll pay thousands."

Aria hesitated. "And he would . . . disseminate . . . these photographs widely? Publish them?"

The man looked at her like she was weird. "Now, what else would he do with them?"

Aria nodded slowly. "Yes. Of course." She looked again at the young Hork-Bajir and repeated thoughtfully, "Yes, of course."

"So let me just ask you, lady, since you're a big nature photographer and all: What is that thing?"

"You don't know?"

Frank shook his head. "This guy comes driving up with this thing lashed in the back of his pickup truck. Says he saw it out wandering around the side of the highway. Asked me what I'd pay for it. I gave him fifty bucks."

"You made a good deal," Aria said. "I'm sure he's worth more than that."

"So what is it, that's what I'd like to know."

Aria shrugged. "I don't know. I've never seen anything like it. But you know, you shouldn't call it a 'freak.'"

"Not politically correct, huh?" Frank said knowingly.

"It's not that," Aria said. "It's just that it's like nothing I've ever seen. No animal I know." She smiled. "You could present it as an alien and no one would be able to dispute you."

"Alien, huh?" Frank nodded. "Hey, that's not a bad idea. Lot of crazy people out there believe in all that UFO, space alien crap."

"Yes. And while you're changing things, maybe you could show a little humanity to these animals. They need bigger cages, more light, more fresh air. At the very least."

"I'll think on that," Frank said with an expression that said he'd do no such thing.

Aria turned and walked away, brushing past Rachel and me. I turned my head away so she wouldn't be able to recognize me later.

We followed Aria at a safe distance, trying to look like we were scoping the caged animals. Aria stepped out into the bright sun and looked around expectantly.

Seconds later, a black limousine came tearing into the dirt parking lot, raising a cloud of dust.

The limo pulled to a stop and the driver jumped out to open the door for her.

I stared with my weak human eyes as she stepped in and sat down. For a moment the door remained open and I could see her as clearly as human eyes would allow.

She was looking in our direction, but could not see us. She was in sunlight and we were in dark shadow.

Aria gazed thoughtfully up at the Frank's Safari sign. There was a flicker of a smile, but no more.

"Who are you?" I whispered.

The driver shut the door and she was gone.

CHAPTER 16

There wasn't a lot of debate back at the barn that evening about what to do with the baby Hork-Bajir.

"We go in and get him," Jake said.

"It could be a trap," Marco pointed out. "This Aria person could still be a Controller. This could all be a setup."

I wanted to ask why a Controller would care about the conditions of the animals in that hideous zoo. But I didn't. I guess I've gotten so I say less and less. Sometimes all the communicating that people do just seems irrelevant. Action is what counts.

Jake nodded. "We have to act on the assumption that this is a trap. We'll divide our forces. Group A goes in, Group B hangs back."

Marco smirked to Rachel. "He's just so *Patton*."

Jake grinned and aimed a punch at Marco's shoulder.

Then followed one of the more bizarre parts of Animorph life: Jake, Rachel, Cassie, and Marco all sat down in the hay of the barn, whipped open their backpacks, and pulled out books and notebooks.

Homework. I guess when you're fully human and a kid, there's just no escaping homework.

Ax looked over Cassie's shoulder at her science textbook. <But that's not true,> he kept muttering. <That's not at all how gravity works.>

I sat comfortably in the rafters and eavesdropped on Jake's homework. I still enjoy reading when I get a chance. Sometimes I'll go to the park or the beach, places where people read out in the open. I'll find a nice updraft or steady breeze, float fifty or sixty feet up, and read over someone's shoulder. I've read a lot of John Grisham and Stephen King and Nora Roberts. Not whole books, unfortunately, but pages and occasionally whole chapters.

Now I sat reading over Jake's shoulder. And when that grew dull, I fluttered over to spy on Rachel's book.

Then, at last, it was time to go.

<If you would really like to understand the laws of motion as they apply at the quantum level, and how they relate to both gravity and what we Andalites call the seventh force, then —>

Cassie laughed and put a hand on Ax's arm. "Ax, it must be hard not having anyone around to discuss things on your level."

He looked disconcerted. <I . . . no, it's not that,> he said lamely.

"Okay, everyone cool with their parents?" Jake asked.

"Yes, all the right lies have been told," Cassie said, shaking her head regretfully. "Everyone is over at someone else's house. As usual."

"Well, this won't take long," Rachel said.

The others morphed to various bird morphs and we flew to Frank's Safari Land. The sign had been changed. It now cried out that Frank's had the first ever actual space alien. It was working. The lot was filled with a dozen cars.

I was in Group A, along with Rachel. We were the two who were familiar with the place. Also with us was Jake. Cassie, Ax, and Marco were backup, ready to come in if things went wrong.

We landed and demorphed just outside the alligator lagoon. It was dark, but not pitch-black. A hint of dying sun still glowed in the west. The moon wasn't out, but the sky was full of stars.

The others demorphed. I waited. I was going to a morph I'd only used once: Hork-Bajir.

Normally I would never use the Hork-Bajir morph. Hork-Bajir are sentient creatures. We have a rule about morphing humans or other free, sentient species. We're not the Yeerks, after all. We don't just go around taking and using the DNA of free people.

But this was a unique case. We needed Bek, the Hork-Bajir child, to come with us willingly. And I knew that Ket Halpak — whose DNA was the basis for my morph — would not object at all.

"Okay," Jake whispered. "One more time. I go in human and turn off the main power switch so we have darkness. Rachel morphs and as soon as the power goes out, she goes in and removes the back wall. Tobias? You stay here in the dark till Rachel says go. Then you run in, snatch the kid, and run back out. Cassie will be ready to take him after that. We get him a quarter-mile down the back road to the cornfield. All clear?"

Rachel winked at me. "You know, Marco's right. He's gotten *so* Patton."

"Oh, shut up," Jake said good-naturedly.

Jake remained human and began to walk carefully around the outer fence of the alligator lagoon.

"Hey, did Jake say knock down *one* wall? Or did he say knock down some walls?" Rachel asked, dripping with fake innocence.

<You know perfectly well he just wants you to get us into that place. He did not say you should knock the whole place down just because Frank is a creep and he mistreats animals,> I said sternly. <On the other hand, it is dark. You might get confused. . . . >

Rachel laughed her slightly insane, ready-for-a-fight laugh. "Yeah. I might."

She began to morph an elephant. Now, earlier when I said it was kind of cool watching Rachel go to eagle? It's not the same, watching her turn into an elephant. There is nothing even slightly attractive about it.

For one thing, there is the way she grows. In sudden lumps of flesh that pop out of her thighs, her stomach, even her head. It is disturbing to see a lump of gray flesh the size of a refrigerator bulge out of the side of someone's head.

She lumped and bumped and glooped her way from being a normal-sized girl to being a shapeless behemoth. Her legs became pillars. So did her arms. Her elephant feet sank into the damp soil.

She was grinning at me when her white teeth seemed to flow together and then sprout out and out like a spear coming at me. They curved up to a point: a pair of tusks.

Her nose began to hang down like it was running, then like it was melting, then it began to thicken and darken and grow. Of course, by then the beach-blanket-sized ears were already formed.

The last part of Rachel to disappear entirely was her hair. For several seconds she looked exactly like an elephant wearing a blond wig.

All this time, I had started morphing as well.

It's strange morphing anything. I mean, no matter what you become it is a nightmare. Just imagine watching your own flesh squirm and melt and wither, shrink or swell. Imagine hearing your own internal organs go watery and squish away. Imagine having body parts you've never had before, and a brain that knows how to use them.

Morphing is always a freak show. But there is a special quality to morphing a nonterrestrial animal. According to Ax, DNA is a very common thing in the galaxy. That same double helix of atoms forms the blueprint for all of life on Earth and almost all life-forms elsewhere.

But beyond that, there aren't a lot of similarities between alien bodies and say, humans. Real life turns out not to be like *Star Trek*. Aliens are not just humans wearing funny ears, nose putty, and costumes.

There is nothing remotely human about a Hork-Bajir. What's weird is there are slight similarities between hawks and Hork-Bajir.

The taloned feet are very much alike. The almost beaklike mouth is similar. And . . . well, that's about it for similarity.

Hork-Bajir are huge. Seven feet tall. Where my bones are hollow and light, theirs are thick and dense as steel. Where my insides are built for digesting raw meat, a fairly simple job, theirs are infinitely more complex to allow them to digest tree bark.

And while I have some natural weapons — beak and talons — the Hork-Bajir *are* a natural weapon. The claws that allow them to climb the skyscraper-sized trees of their home world, the wrist and elbow and forehead blades that allow them to scrape the bark from those trees, can all be used as weapons.

But the Hork-Bajir had never used them as weapons until the Yeerks and the Andalites brought their war to the Hork-Bajir world.

I grew and grew. Grew till I could almost look Rachel straight in the eye.

My talons became Tyrannosaurus feet. My mouth grew teeth, sharp ones for cutting bark and serrated molars for grinding it up.

My wings lost their feathers and extended out and out. Hands grew where my "finger" bones had been. Muscle covered my entire body. And from that muscle the bony projections of blades grew.

<Well, we're a nice-looking couple,> Rachel said. <Let's go to the dance.>

I heard a noise. Car engines racing, brakes screeching. Then car doors slamming. Several. Many. I shot a look toward the parking lot, but it was mostly blocked from view.

And at that moment the lights of Frank's Safari Land went out.

<Show time,> Rachel said and laughed her wild laugh.

CHAPTER 17

Out went the lights and I quickly discovered that Hork-Bajir don't have much in the way of night vision. Neither do elephants. But elephants don't care all that much, since they can pretty well stomp anything that gets in their way.

HhhrrrEEEEE-uh! Rachel trumpeted and took off around the perimeter of the alligator lagoon, heading for Frank's Safari Land.

I was amazed how fast she was. I could barely keep up.

I heard annoyed yelling coming from the building.

"Hey, turn on the lights!"

"I want my money back!"

We rushed at the closest wall. Rachel came to a stop and carefully pressed the flat front of her wrecking-ball head against it. She leaned her weight forward and we both heard a creaking sound.

<Heh-heh-heh,> she cackled. <Just wood. Doesn't this little piggy know he should build his house out of brick? Come out, come out, little piggy! Or I'll huff, and I'll puff, and I'll crush this dump like a matchbox!>

She reared back and slammed her weight forward.

WHAM! CRRRRREEEK!

<That should have gotten people to step back,> she said. <Now we go in.>

She backed up three elephant steps and lunged forward, hurtling her dump truck weight against the flimsy wooden wall.

WHAM! Crrrr-ACK! Crunch!

WHOOOMPF! The wall fell in.

Now people were really yelling. "Hey, I'm getting outta here!"

Rachel happily stomped in across the shattered timbers and splintered plywood, trumpeting like mad, swinging her big trunk back and forth and generally making the kind of destructive mess she loved to make.

<Everybody out!> she ordered in wide-band

thought-speak. <Rabid elephant! Psycho elephant on the loose! It's Dumbo-zilla!>

In the general panic, no one would recall that they didn't really "hear" anyone shout that warning.

I followed gingerly in Rachel's wake. She was busily tossing her trunk up and down, making the low ceiling jump with each impact.

I squeezed past her and searched for the little lost Hork-Bajir. I found him in his cage.

But I was not alone.

On the other side of the cage stood three men. Two carried standard handguns. The third carried a weapon I'd seen far too often before: a Yeerk Dracon beam.

The three human-Controllers gaped at me. Not the way actual humans would react to suddenly encountering a Hork-Bajir. But the way people already familiar with Hork-Bajir would react to seeing one where he wasn't expected.

<Uh, Rachel?> I said.

<What? Sorry, I'm all turned around and can't help stomping this place to pieces.>

<Save that for Jake,> I said. <We have company.>

"Who are you?" one of the men demanded. "Visser Three didn't tell us that . . . wait! It's one of the renegade Hork-Bajir! One of the escaped hosts!"

Bek looked at me pleadingly. The Controllers leveled their weapons at me. And one of them began yelling into a watch that must have also been a communicator.

This was going to get ugly fast. They were here to grab the baby Hork-Bajir. So were we. One big difference: They might not care if Bek lived or died.

CHAPTER 18

"So, a renegade Hork-Bajir," one of the Controllers said. "Let's grab them both! Visser Three will be very pleased." He raised his Dracon beam and leveled it at me. "You can make it easy or hard, Hork-Bajir."

Bek was between them and me. If I attacked . . .

Fortunately, I was not alone.

I never even saw the wolf till it was on the Controller. Its big jaws clamped down tight over his gun hand.

"Aaaahhhh!" he screamed.

<Cassie? Good timing!>

<Yeah, it's me, but don't just stand there. There are more coming! Lots more!>

I didn't hesitate a second longer. I leaped over Bek's cage and landed, T-rex feetfirst, on one of the men. Hork-Bajir may not be geniuses for the most part, but they are quick.

My victim went down, yelling and scrambling to get away.

BLAM! The gunshot was so close the sound hurt worse than the bullet. The bullet knocked a neat, round hole in my left elbow blade.

I slashed instinctively. The gun dropped to the floor. And the Controller would now have a hard time counting past eight on his fingers.

We had a momentary advantage, Cassie and I. I fumbled with clumsy Hork-Bajir fingers at the lock on Bek's cage. Then something black, shaggy, and massive pushed by me.

<Here. Let Gorilla-boy do that for you,> Marco said. <See, it requires delicacy, patience, a subtle touch.>

He grabbed the front of the cage, twining his sausage fingers through the bars and . . .

RRRIIPP!

He tore the cage open like a bag of chips.

<Come with me, Bek,> I said to the terrified Hork-Bajir baby.

<Ket Halpak?>

<Um . . . yes. Come.>

He took my hand, and that's when everything broke loose.

BLAM! BLAM! BLAM!

TSEEWW! TSEEWW!

The blinding light of muzzle flashes and even more blinding Dracon beams. Explosions that rocked the room.

Suddenly, an elephant.

Suddenly faces, angry, frightened faces visible in the flash of gunfire.

I felt as if someone had punched me in the stomach. For a moment I was confused. Had Bek hit me? No. A bullet! I could see the hole. I could see the blood.

Hrrreee-YAH! Rachel trumpeted.

And now there were more creatures. The lynx, loose from its cage. A tiger, roaring, rushing, slashing.

A gorilla, swinging fists the size of canned hams.

An Andalite, his tail flying like a bullwhip, slashing with terrible accuracy.

The attack was reckless, desperate, heedless. Bullets flying! Dracon beams burning holes in cages and walls. Flames rising around me. Smoke.

I clutched Bek's hand and staggered back, looking for an escape route. But it was pretty dark aside from the angry weapon's flashes. The ceiling was sloping down in places where it had almost fallen. Walls were twisted. Cages were strewn here and there. Animals screamed. Human voices shouted.

The pain hit suddenly. Late, but not forgotten. I doubled over, but kept my grip on Bek's hand. He was yanking, tugging, pulling in panic.

Now the battle was becoming more organized. The Controllers had the front half of the building, and more were around the back, splashing hurriedly through the alligator lagoon to cut us off.

Rachel was demorphing. Her elephant bulk was doing more harm than good. As she shrank toward human she ducked out of sight and faded into the dark.

The Controllers — there must have been a dozen by now — had learned a little humility. They were cowering behind cover, shooting wildly around corners, waiting, no doubt, for our retreat to be cut off.

<Tobias! Get that kid out of here!> Jake yelled.

<You need me,> I gasped.

<Get. Him. Out!>

I grabbed Bek more tightly and began to back toward the crushed wall we'd come through. The pain in my stomach felt like someone had shoved a red-hot sword into me.

I felt a cool breeze on my back. I turned, ready to plunge through the opening into the night beyond. But the way was not clear.

An Andalite stood there.

He was older than Ax, larger, battle-scarred. He exuded a darkness that was blacker than the night. A darkness that came from the twisted, evil slug that lived inside that captive Andalite brain.

Visser Three!

He whipped his Andalite tail forward, and I stepped back. But even as I registered the Andalite body that had once belonged to a powerful Andalite war-prince, I began to see the changes.

He was morphing. Visser Three, the only Andalite-Controller. The only Yeerk with the power to morph.

Visser Three, who had traveled the galaxy acquiring morphs of the most deadly creatures of the known universe.

<Ah, a renegade Hork-Bajir,> he said, sounding delighted. <The little runaway and the renegade. Ket Halpak, if I am not mistaken. Well, my Hork-Bajir friend, I'll soon have you back at the Yeerk pool. You'll soon belong to us again.>

CHAPTER 19

<Poor, stupid Hork-Bajir,> Visser Three said, dripping fake pity. <You can't even appreciate the magnificence of this morph. It's called a *Kaftid*.>

The Visser's Andalite head narrowed and stretched forward till it looked like the head of a seahorse. You know, with that rigid, tubular mouth? His neck elongated. Two leathery wings that could not possibly have allowed him to fly grew just behind the head.

His four-legged body mutated, growing a fifth, sixth, seventh, eighth leg! The tail disappeared altogether, and where there had been blue fur highlighted with tan, there was now a green, slimy, froglike skin.

I yanked Bek close, fought a wave of pain, and tried to dodge around the monster that Visser Three was becoming. But Bek was in full panic. He was yelping and crying and trying to get back to what probably seemed like the safety of the building.

I tried to lift him up but I was unfamiliar with my Hork-Bajir body, and worried about cutting the young Hork-Bajir with my blades.

At last I managed to get an arm around Bek's middle and ran around the Visser's right side.

Too late!

SssssPASSSS!

A liquid the color of antifreeze squirted from the monster's pouting mouth. It missed me by millimeters and hit a fallen two-by-four.

Hsssssss!

Acid! In seconds the wood was smoking and disintegrating from the corrosion of the greenish-yellow acid.

<Hah-hah-hah!> Visser Three exulted. <Are you ready to surrender, Hork-Bajir? You're not a fighter! Your people were meant to be our slaves!>

Surrender. What an excellent idea. With Bek in my arms, I couldn't risk a direct attack on this hideous, acid-spitting alien freak.

"I surrender!" I cried.

<Down on your face, then,> he snapped. <I

have Andalite bandits to deal with. Down on your face in the mud, slave. And keep hold of that little one, too.>

"Yes. Down on face," I said, trying my best to sound like a Hork-Bajir. I knelt and started to stretch out. And that's when Visser Three got overanxious. He started to rush past me, desperate to reach the others.

He stepped a little too near. And suddenly, instead of eight legs, he had five. One fast, powerful swipe of my arm. Blade! Blade! Blade! I was like that new three-blade razor.

<Arrggghhh!> he bellowed in pain and rage. He began to topple over, unable to support himself with his one left leg. But even as he fell, he twisted his head and took aim. Point-blank range.

Point-blank at Bek.

Jerking every muscle in my body, I rolled over Bek, putting my back between him and the Visser's acid spray.

Pain! Unimaginable pain! I was burning alive! I was on fire!

I couldn't think, couldn't control myself, not even for a moment.

I got to my feet, staggered, screaming in agony, to the lagoon, and plunged into the water.

Water. Blessed, muddy water diluted the acid before it could eat right through my spine.

Relief!

But even as I shuddered at the lessening of the pain, I realized that I had let Bek go. I rose up from the lagoon, dripping mud, and looked frantically toward shore.

No Visser Three. No *Kaftid*.

And no Bek.

<Nooooo!> I cried in anguish.

From the wreckage of Frank's Safari Land came a burly, deceptively roly-poly animal. It ran to the water's edge and stopped. It reared up to its full height, as tall as a Hork-Bajir.

The grizzly bear blinked nearsightedly. <Tobias?>

<I lost Bek!>

<Get out of that water or you'll lose your butt!> Rachel yelled. <You've got gators coming after you!>

<I lost Bek!> I cried.

<Forget him,> she said harshly. <The Yeerks are bailing. So are we. There's cops and fire engines and paramedics coming. We're out of here!>

CHAPTER 20

I had lost the young Hork-Bajir. The Yeerks had him. I had lost him.

Maybe they'd get him to reveal the way to the secret Hork-Bajir valley. Maybe.

Maybe they'd make him a Controller. All because of me. Because I'd let pain distract me. Because I wasn't focused.

That had been the human in me. The human in me had given too much weight to pain. A hawk knew better. A hawk didn't care about pain.

I was in my meadow. The sun was just coming up, rising to hide behind the gray blanket drawn across the sky during the night.

I was ravenous.

And why? Why had I not eaten? The human in

me. How else to explain the strange confusion I felt, the horrific visions of myself as my own prey?

Human.

I could become human again. Right now I could do it. Right now I could tick off the two hours and never, never have to kill to eat. Well . . . at least not have to do my own killing.

A quick morph, two hours, and I'd be back. Back where I'd started. Human. Tobias the boy.

Ever since the Ellimist had given me back my power to morph and allowed me to reacquire my own original DNA, the question had hung in the air. Rachel wondered, I know. Once she'd suggested it to me: Why not just become fully human again?

I hadn't given her an answer.

I saw the other hawk float suddenly into my field of vision. He was getting bolder. More aggressive. How long till he attacked and I withdrew? If I'd been a true hawk, the battle would long since have been drawn. Even an old, sick hawk would have put up a better fight than I had so far.

He was floating above the rabbit hole. My rabbit hole. He was pure hawk. The real thing. Not some freak with a talon in one world and a foot in the other.

<Hey there,> I thought-spoke. <Yeah, you.

Hawk. Why don't you go pick on someone else's territory?>

No answer. Of course not. Words meant nothing to him. They weren't even background noise. They might as well have been silence.

<Those are my rabbits, you jerk. Get out of here. I know I don't eat them, but they're still mine. I know I'm unable to hunt and kill like a hawk should, but do you have to rub my nose in it? My beak?>

The hunger came up in a wave.

What a sickening life. What a disgusting creature I was. To live my life as a hawk, I had to fight another hawk. A bird fight. And over what? A rabbit? A few mice? I was going to fight that bird for the right to kill and eat rodents?

Before, I'd had no choice. Now I did. I was choosing to live as a hawk. Choosing to build a life around a scruffy meadow and the pitiful rodents in it.

Maybe I was crazy.

Before, I'd been able to tell myself I had nowhere else to go. No one to take me in. No parents. No family. Now there was this Aria person. She was actually going out of her way to find me, to care for me.

Maybe.

<Tobias?>

I jerked, startled. I recognized Ax's thought-speak voice and calmed down. He comes around sometimes. We are the weird couple of the galaxy: the alien and the Bird-boy.

<Hey, Ax-man, what's up?>

<Up is the opposite of down. Although, of course, those terms are meaningless outside the context of a distinct, localized gravity field.>

<Ooookay.>

<Was that funny? I was attempting a joke.>

<Ah. Well . . . I'm probably not the guy to ask,> I said evasively.

I looked down from my perch on the eerie-looking creature who was my friend. When you look at an Andalite, there's just no avoiding the obvious: They aren't from around here. He was looking up at me with one stalk eye. The other was roaming left and right, while his main eyes gazed out across the meadow.

<Have you eaten?> he asked.

I could lie. <No.>

<There is insufficient prey?>

<Yeah. And one too many predators.>

<Yes, I saw the other member of your species.>

<I have no species,> I said. <I'm a one-of-a-kind freak.>

Ax didn't have an answer for that. I don't

think Andalites approve of self-pity or other pointless emotions like that.

I sighed. <Sorry. I'm hungry and in a bad mood.>

<Hunger is distracting,> Ax allowed. <Since the others are in their human school today, I thought perhaps we could investigate this Aria woman some more.>

<We should be finding that little Hork-Bajir I lost,> I said bitterly. <Not checking out my relatives.>

<You found the Hork-Bajir the first time by following the Aria woman.>

Was he implying something? No. It was just coincidence, wasn't it? Aria was a nature photographer. She'd heard about this strange animal and had gone to see it. She couldn't be a Controller. Why would a Controller complain about the treatment of animals at Frank's Safari Land?

<Okay, Ax-man. It'll give us something to do, anyway.>

I took a last look at my opponent. <Go ahead,> I said to him. <Go ahead, take the stupid meadow.>

CHAPTER 21

We took turns, Ax and I. He used the roofs of the skyscrapers to demorph and remorph. Out of sight of curious eyes.

All that day a red-tailed hawk and a northern harrier flew around the Hyatt Regency Hotel. When Aria went to lunch down the street, we followed. When she visited an exhibit of black-and-white photographs, I morphed to human and stayed with her.

We followed her. Hour after hour. Waiting, watching for some contact with a known Controller. Looking for any attempt to visit the Yeerk pool hidden beneath a large part of our town.

A Yeerk must return to the Yeerk pool every

three days. We couldn't watch her for three days, but we could watch her for a lot of that time.

She didn't.

Instead, after eight hours of watching, we had seen her eat, seen her read the newspaper, seen her walk in the park, seen her return to the hotel several times and go back out again.

No one had approached her.

We'd learned nothing. Nothing at all, except that she seemed to enjoy her hotel room. She'd go out for a while, but return every couple of hours. She'd leave the curtains open. We could watch her, except for when she stepped into the bathroom and closed the door.

<What is beyond that door?> Ax asked.

<Toilet,> I said. <You know. Peeing and so on.>

<Ah. Are there no . . . no toilet facilities except in the hotel?> Ax wondered.

<Sure there are. But, you know, I think women are more iffy about using public rest rooms than guys are.>

<Why?>

<Well, I don't know. It's probably the whole sitting down versus standing up thing.>

Ax had no idea what I was talking about. But I guess he figured he'd let it go. Besides, having made her pit stop, Aria was on the move again.

We caught up with her outside. She was walking quickly along the sidewalk. It was maybe three in the afternoon now. Time for us to be getting back to hook up with Jake and the others.

And that's when it happened. A little girl broke away from her mother, turned around, and went running back into the street. A city bus was barreling straight toward her.

<Look out!> I yelled out of sheer instinct.

There was a scream from the mother. But she was too far away.

I saw Aria's head snap around. She saw the accident about to happen. She dropped her camera and made a tackle-the-runner-on-the-two-yard-line lunge.

She hit the girl in the back, knocked her forward, and rolled with the little girl onto the narrow concrete median strip.

The mother came running. The little girl bellowed, but seemed okay. Aria got up and brushed herself off.

<She just saved that little girl's life,> I said.

<Yes. And she could easily have been killed.>

<Oh, my God,> I said slowly, amazed. <She really is human. No Controller would ever have done that!>

<No,> Ax agreed. <That makes it very clear that Aria is not acting as a Controller would. Very clear.>

Something in Ax's choice of words bothered

me, but I forgot about it in the rush of emotions that followed.

I'd been assuming this was all a trap. I'd assumed Aria was a Controller.

But she wasn't. She was what she said she was. A human woman looking for her long-lost cousin Tobias.

My last excuse for remaining a hawk, for refusing to become human again, was lost. Now I *could* have a home. Now I *could* have a family.

True. All of it true.

I could have a home. Like a human being. A home!

I would not kill my breakfast. I would not eat roadkill. I would sleep in a bed. And Rachel would look at me without having to hide the pity in her eyes.

CHAPTER 22

I flew to Rachel's room that night. I couldn't sleep. And I was literally starving. But the last thing I could think about was hunting.

She'd gone to sleep early but had left the window open. I fluttered in and landed on her desk. When I realized she was asleep, I started to leave.

"No, wait. Don't go," she said, rubbing the sleep out of her eyes and sitting up. She did not turn on a light. I was relieved somehow.

"You missed the meeting," Rachel said.

<Yeah. Sorry. What did you guys decide to do about Bek?>

Rachel tousled her hair. "Jake came up with the idea that the Yeerks would probably try to use him to trap the other free Hork-Bajir."

105

<Yeah?>

"This facility the Hork-Bajir wouldn't tell you about? The one where they've been raiding to free other Hork-Bajir? Jake figures they'll take Bek there. As bait."

<Or at least that's what Jake wants to believe,> I said resentfully. <Jara and Ket and Toby trusted me with that information. Maybe Jake's just looking for an excuse to squeeze the Hork-Bajir to reveal this place to us.>

Rachel looked at me like she was going to argue. Then she kind of laughed. "Maybe. Jake *has* gotten more subtle. It doesn't matter. We don't have another lead. Either Bek is at this site or he's down in the Yeerk pool or he's dead. In any case, we're going in tomorrow in broad daylight. School's out for a teacher conference."

I cringed. <I told Jara and Ket and Toby I'd get that little Hork-Bajir back.>

"We almost did. It's not your fault the Yeerks got him."

I let that go. It was my fault, but there was no point in the two of us going "yes it was, no it wasn't" all night.

<Ax and I followed that Aria woman.> I said.

"Yeah, Ax mentioned that."

<I — I think she may be for real. Not that it matters, really. I mean, you know . . .>

Rachel climbed out of bed and came over to sit at the desk close to me. "Of course it matters, Tobias. She's family. And she wants to take care of you."

I forced a laugh. <Yeah, that'll work out real well. "Hi, Cousin Aria. It's me, Tobias. No, over here: the bird. Yes, your cousin is a red-tailed hawk. Surprise!">

"You don't *have* to be."

I pretended not to know what she was talking about. <What?>

"Tobias, you have the power to become human again. Fully human."

<Uh-huh.>

"You can go to this woman as a human. You can be Tobias again. You can have a family. Someone around to take care of you."

<I don't need anyone to take care of me.> I bristled.

Rachel jumped up suddenly. "Tobias, don't play dumb! You know what I mean. You think I don't know that you're going hungry? I can look at you and see it. Something is wrong lately. I mean, I saw you — never mind."

My heart was in my throat. <What?!> I almost screamed. <You saw me what? Eat that . . . that roadkill? How is that any different than what you do? Or any human? You go to the supermarket

107

and buy beef or pork or chicken that's been dead for weeks!>

"I don't care that you ate roadkill. Stop being an idiot! I care about *you*. And when I see you doing that, I know things are going wrong for you. But you're off in your own little hawk world and no one is allowed to help you. You'd rather starve than ask for help. You can't ever admit that your life may suck because then you'll feel weak."

<I'm a hawk,> I snapped. <A bird of prey. When we're weak, we die. That's the law for us. I'm not a human being. Not anymore. No one helps a hawk. A hawk lives by his eyes and wings and talons.>

"You're a hawk?" Rachel sneered. "You *talk*, Tobias. You *read*. You have *emotions*. Those are human things, not hawk things."

<I know! I know! Don't you think I know? That's why I'm going hungry. Because I'm not hawk enough. That's why I let Bek get away, because I was human enough to care more about my pain and fear than I cared about doing what I had to do.>

"That's just stupid," Rachel said angrily. "It doesn't even make sense. You know what? You have to make a choice, Tobias. You can be a hawk. But you will never, ever, not in a million years, be a pure, true hawk. If you want to stay a hawk you'll be like you are now: confused, conflicted, torn up inside, never knowing what you really are. Or . . . or you can be human again. All human. You can live with the Aria woman and eat at the table and sleep in a bed."

<And never fly,> I said. <Never fly again. Never see with hawk's eyes. Never morph again. I know you guys would all be nice to me, but I'd lose all of you. I'd lose being an Animorph.>

"You wouldn't lose *me*," Rachel said.

For a long while neither of us spoke. Then Rachel, in a whisper, said, "What am I supposed to do, Tobias? I'm a girl. You're a bird. This is way past Romeo and Juliet, Montagues and Capulets. This isn't Kate Winslet and Leo DiCaprio coming from different social groups or whatever. It's not like you're black and I'm white like Cassie and Jake. No one but a moron cares about that. We are . . . we can't hold hands, Tobias. We can't dance. We can't go to a movie together."

<I . . . God, Rachel, don't you think I know all that? Don't you think I want to have all that? But I can't keep changing. I can't keep becoming something different.>

"One more change, Tobias. Back to human. You'd be free of this stupid war and free of all the danger of living as a hawk. I wouldn't have to worry about you anymore."

I couldn't take anymore. I just couldn't. It was too much. I felt like I'd explode if I didn't get away from her. I couldn't be that near to her . . . couldn't.

I turned and prepared to fly.

"Tobias. It's tomorrow, by the way. Your birthday. I had Marco hack into the school records. It's tomorrow you have to see the lawyer and Aria. Whatever happens there — whatever you decide — come see me afterward, okay? Maybe we can have a cake with a candle."

I spread my wings and flew away.

CHAPTER 23

I didn't sleep a lot that night. Talking to Rachel had not exactly made me feel peaceful.

In the morning, in a couple of hours, we would all go to the Hork-Bajir. I would ask them where the secret Yeerk facility was. We would tell them that's where the Yeerks had Bek. Maybe that would even be the truth.

There would be a battle. Maybe we'd survive and maybe not.

And then I would have a different battle to fight. One with myself.

Human or hawk? What was I?

I sat in my tree and clutched my perch and stared out across the meadow. The hunger was terrible now. Terrible enough to leave me weak. If

I didn't eat I would not have the strength to fly to the Hork-Bajir. I would not make it to the battle.

Was that so important? Hadn't I done enough? Hadn't I paid a high enough price?

I could morph to human. Stay human. Eat as a human. No fighting over territory, no fighting Yeerks.

And I would still have Rachel.

Such a simple decision. So easy. Any fool knew the answer. Be human! Be human!

I spotted the slight movement of grass in the dim predawn light. The rabbit coming out to feed. So cautious now. She'd lost one baby.

Then I saw the other hawk. He was waiting. he was watching me. And I knew right then today was the day. He could see my weakness. He knew he could take me.

I began to shake. To tremble. Some combination of hunger and fear and emotions too numerous to list.

I saw the rabbits clearly. They were mine for the taking. But I knew the terrible vision that awaited me. I knew that as I descended on my prey I would become that prey.

It was the human in me. I had to fight it! If I wanted to be a hawk, I had to destroy the part of me that felt, the part of me that cried for the creatures I killed. No predator could feel for his prey. I could not allow myself to feel the terror I inflicted, feel the pain I caused.

<That does it,> I told the other hawk. <This is stupid. I'm not fighting you! I'm not going to kill those helpless creatures. I'm done with this. I'm a human being!>

I fluttered to the ground. And I began to morph.

Morph to human!

No. Not yet, I told myself. *The others are counting on me still. The Hork-Bajir are counting on me. Later. After the battle. Then I can morph to human and go to Aria.*

I flapped my wings and rose into the air. I needed food and I had seen a cat killed by a passing car. Just this one last time. Then I would put it all behind me.

One last time, picking the dead animal flesh from the pavement. One last humiliation, one last battle, and I would be done forever.

It was my birthday, after all. A good day to be reborn.

I found the cat. I ate as much of it as I could hold.

CHAPTER 24

We, the Animorphs, stood before the free Hork-Bajir. I rested on a low branch and did the talking. I told them about our failed rescue attempt. I explained our guess that Bek was at whatever facility the Hork-Bajir had been raiding.

"A trap," Toby said.

<Yes.>

"And you want to step into that trap, anyway?"

<We have no choice. We *will* free Bek. We only need you to tell us the exact location of this facility.>

Toby considered this for a moment. Even now it was weird talking to a Hork-Bajir who could think and speak on my level. And maybe a little over my level at times.

"We will go with you," Toby said.

"No, no," Jake said. "We work alone. Besides, we're just going to grab one little Hork-Bajir. We don't need a whole army."

Toby said, "This is a trap. But it is a trap because the Yeerks expect us to come after Bek. We must do the unexpected. We must surprise them even as we step into their trap."

I looked at Jake. Jake raised an eyebrow at me in surprise.

<I told you: Toby ain't your average Hork-Bajir,> I said to Jake in private thought-speak.

"The Yeerks expect a rescue mission. Or at worst, a raid like the ones we have carried out: stealthy, in and out, quickly disappearing into the forest," Toby explained.

"What do you want instead?" Jake asked her.

Toby got a hard look in her eyes. "Attack! Destroy the entire facility. Even if it means destroying other Hork-Bajir. Even if it means losing Bek."

Even I was shocked. <That's awfully harsh, Toby.>

She smiled grimly. "The Yeerks must not be allowed to think that they can use hostages against us."

"Aren't you kind of missing the point?" Cassie said quietly. "I thought the point was to save Bek."

"No," Toby said. "The point is to defeat the Yeerks. We must be strong. Once we free a Hork-Bajir, he must never be taken again."

"Do you think the Yeerks will respect you? They won't. They'll come after you harder," Cassie pointed out.

Toby nodded. "That is true. But the Hork-Bajir will respect *themselves*. A fool is strong so that others will see. A wise person is strong for himself. The Hork-Bajir will be strong for the Hork-Bajir. That way, when the Yeerks are all gone, we will still be strong."

"Fair enough," Jake said.

Marco stepped forward and jerked his thumb at Rachel. "Toby, meet Rachel. You two can visit the psychiatrist together."

"She's right," Rachel said. "Someone pushes you, you push back. Doesn't matter who it is. You have to make the other guy pay a price."

Cassie rolled her eyes. "That's like a perfect rationalization for gang warfare."

"World War Two," Rachel shot back. "The Nazis push, you push back. If you don't, they kill you anyway."

"Northern Ireland? The Middle East?" Cassie said.

Marco said, "They shend one of yoursh to the hoshpital, you shend one of theirsh to the morgue. That's the Chicago way."

Cassie and Rachel both just stared at him.

"Sean Connery in *The Untouchables*," he said, disbelieving. "C'mon, don't you people have cable?"

"Ah, Sean Connery. I thought you were doing Urkel," Cassie teased.

"Marco *is* Urkel," Rachel said.

It took Toby just minutes to assemble the Hork-Bajir. Ten of them ended up coming with us. More would have come but we insisted some be left behind. Just in case.

Ten Hork-Bajir and the six of us. Not exactly an army. But not exactly a group to laugh at, either.

If I went through with my decision to become human, it would be my last battle.

We traveled along the valley to its farthest end. It was a good walk. The valley was big enough to house a lot more Hork-Bajir. The El-limist had been looking ahead when he'd chosen it.

"I fight you," a Hork-Bajir I didn't know said to me as I fluttered along, keeping pace with the group.

<What?>

"In Yeerk pool. Before. I fight you." He grinned

and pointed to a nasty scar across his left eye. Then he pantomimed a bird coming down and raking his face with its talons. "Fal Tagut say 'Aaaahhhh!' "

<I did that? I'm . . . sorry.>

"No sorry! Fal Tagut not free." He tapped his head with one long claw. "Fal Tagut have Yeerk. Now free. Good! Hork-Bajir and humans friends. Toby say."

It was a long speech for a Hork-Bajir. Fal Tagut seemed worn out by it.

I wondered about the image of Hork-Bajir and humans living side by side if the Yeerks were defeated. Humans didn't have a great record of getting along with people different from themselves. Humans killed one another over skin color or eye shape or because they prayed differently to the same god. Hard to imagine humans welcoming seven-foot-tall goblins into the local Boy Scout troop when they couldn't even manage to tolerate some gay kid.

Get pushed, push back. Toby had already seen it. She knew that the Hork-Bajir would need to be strong to defend themselves against humans once the Yeerks were defeated.

Get pushed, push back. The only way.

No, not the *only* way. There was another way. Don't push to begin with. It's the aggressors who start the cycle. It's the guy who wakes up in the morning and decides he can't get through the day without finding someone to attack, to insult, to hurt.

But where does that leave you? Letting jerks dictate your reactions? Always sinking to the level of whatever creep comes along?

My mind went to that other hawk. The one who wanted my territory. There it was: Push and push back. But it wasn't a good comparison, was it? That hawk wasn't human. All he had was instinct. Couldn't blame him for doing what was natural.

So maybe humans were no better. Maybe you couldn't blame a human animal for just being an animal. Except that my hawk opponent had no choice, no free will. He'd never heard "Blessed are the peacemakers," or "I have a dream," or "All men are created equal."

It suddenly occurred to me, right then, for the first time, that what I thought was so unique about me — that I was half instinctive predator, and half human being — wasn't so unique after all.

Every human — Jake, Rachel, Marco, Cassie, all humans — kind of lives on that edge between savage and saint. And the thing is that sometimes when you get pushed you do have to push back. And other times, you have to turn the other cheek.

119

I saw the scar on Fal Tagut's face. I'd put it there. I'd been trying to kill him at the time because he'd been trying to kill me. Now we were on the same side.

I guess the trick is to figure out when to do which thing. When to fight, when to let up. A balancing act. And even if I went back to being fully human in body and mind, that balancing act wouldn't go away.

Maybe realizing that should have made me feel bad. But it didn't. Just made me feel human.

CHAPTER 25

<It is a ground-based weapons platform,> Ax said. He was struggling to keep the slow-burn anger out of his voice. <You can see the Dracon beam already in place. They only need to position the targeting sensors to have it operational.>

We were at the edge of a perfectly round bowl blasted or cut into the earth. We were in dense forest. And anyone approaching from air or land would have still seen dense forest. Hologram projectors maintained perfect illusion. Until you got close enough.

Hikers or campers who got close enough would most likely never return. They'd be dispatched by the patrols of human-Controllers and Hork-Bajir.

A patrol had intercepted us. Now they wished they hadn't. The human-Controllers were trussed up tightly and hanging from a very high branch of a very tall tree. The Hork-Bajir may not be rocket scientists, but they are very good with vines, roots, and trees in general. Those Controllers weren't going anywhere for a while.

The Hork-Bajir-Controllers, four of them, had been knocked unconscious, their faces shoved into dug-out holes in the dirt. Apparently, this kept Hork-Bajir unconscious longer. These four would be coming with us. Unwillingly at first. But in three days or less, when the Yeerks in their heads died for lack of Kandrona rays, there'd be four more free Hork-Bajir.

We had slipped through the hologram and could now peer down cautiously from the lip of the vast hole the Yeerks had made. In the center was a single structure. It looked like some power station or something. Blank steel and bits of this and that jutting out at odd angles. Atop this structure was something that looked like a miniature Washington Monument mounted on a swivel base.

<Is that the Dracon beam? I've never seen one that large,> I said.

Ax swiveled his stalk eyes toward me. <The size is embarrassing, really. If the Yeerks were

any good at engineering they could have an equally powerful weapon a third of that size.>

<Is it powerful?>

<It could vaporize entire mountains on your moon,> he said flatly. <Or destroy an Andalite ship in orbit.>

"Can it be pointed down? At the ground?" Jake asked him.

Ax peered closely at the weapon. Then he smiled that strange Andalite smile they do without a mouth. <Yes.>

"How do we get down there?" Rachel wondered.

"Fly? They'd see us and shoot us out of the air," Cassie said.

<What would they do if they captured a bunch of free Hork-Bajir?> I wondered.

Toby looked at me and nodded. "They would cage us and hold us till we could be made into Controllers again. Until they could transport us to the Yeerk pool."

"They know we were at Frank's Safari Land the other night," Marco pointed out. "So they know we have some contact with the free Hork-Bajir. And if they brought Bek here it means they're expecting a rescue attempt."

"Well, Visser Three knows we're connected to the free Hork-Bajir. But does whoever is running this project know it?" Cassie speculated. "Maybe. Maybe not."

Jake asked Toby, "When you've raided this place in the past, how many of your people have come on each mission?"

"Usually three or four. We did not want to risk everyone."

Jake smiled. "Then we send in three or four Hork-Bajir. It'll look exactly like previous raids. Only these four Hork-Bajir will have hitchhikers on board. They put up a fight, then let themselves be taken. Only then do we demorph and strike."

Marco groaned. "We're not talking fleas again, are we? I hate morphing fleas."

He had good reason. Marco had come very close to being trapped in flea morph. Being trapped as a hawk is one thing. But a flea? I'd rather die.

"Pick a bug, any bug," Rachel said with a laugh. "Flea, fly, mosquito. A bug's a bug."

"Yeah, right," Marco muttered. "I'm an ant and I get chomped in half, I'm a flea and I almost get stuck in morph. I don't have a good record with bugs."

"I got slapped as a fly," Jake offered, like that was helpful.

In the end, after some debate, four Hork-Bajir headed stealthily down toward the secret Yeerk facility. On board them was a collection of insects. A flea, a mosquito, two cockroaches, one housefly, and a wolf spider. Marco was the spider.

I went ahead and did the flea morph. They're gross, mostly blind, bloodsucking, brainless little things, but have you ever tried to kill one? You could swat it all day and it would just laugh.

Unfortunately, I couldn't see anything from my vantage point at the base of Jara Hamee's front horn. I mean nothing. But I could listen to a running, thought-speak description courtesy of Marco. He, after all, had eight eyes.

<Okay, we're sneaking.>

A few minutes later: <I think we see Bek. He's in a cage, right out in the open. But no one's guarding him.>

Then, <Man, the Yeerks have no respect for the Hork-Bajir. I mean, a two-year-old would look at this and think "trap!" Come on, put some effort into it. Post some expendable guards. Something.>

I felt a sudden, violent jerk that translated itself up through Jara Hamee's body. <Let me guess. We're caught.>

<Yep. We are caught,> Marco said, sounding satisfied.

CHAPTER 26

<Okay, here's the deal, as well as I can tell with a mix of simple and compound eyes,> Marco reported. <We're in a cage. Big, thick bars. But a very conventional lock. A human lock. Bek's here, hugging Jara Hamee.>

<How strong are the bars?> Cassie wondered.

<How strong would *you* make the bars if you wanted to lock up Hork-Bajir?> Marco asked.

<Ah. Strong, then.>

<We need to unlock the lock,> Marco said.

<Do you think?> Rachel mocked. <With your intellect, maybe you could be our "seer.">

<Hah. Hah. And also, hah,> Marco said.

<We need the Hork-Bajir to hide whoever demorphs,> Jake said.

<That'd be me,> I said. <I'm smallest. Easiest to hide.>

No one argued. It was obviously true. I fired my springy flea legs and hurtled, somersaulting into the air. I fell for what felt like a very, very long time. Then I hit.

Pht!

I had probably just fallen a thousand times my own height. The equivalent of a human being leaping off a building five times the height of the World Trade Center. And when I hit it was like, "Okay, what's next?"

I began to demorph. Very slowly. I grew to about an inch across, then stopped. <Jara Hamee? Do you see me?>

"Jara sees bug."

<That's me.>

"Tobias? Tobias is bug?"

I found myself wishing we had let Toby come along. Although she was too valuable to risk.

<Yes. I am the bug. Jara? You have to get the other Hork-Bajir to hide me. Form a circle around me.>

"Jara do."

I demorphed some more. Till I was a six-inch monster with pinfeathers growing out of rust-red flea armor. Not a pretty sight. Trust me. You don't want to see what a cross between a hawk beak and a skin-piercing, bloodsucking flea mouthpart looks like.

But I had eyes now. Dim, weak ones, but eyes. I looked around and sighed.

<No, Jara. You want to turn outward. This way it's kind of obvious you're shielding something.>

The Hork-Bajir turned outward and I finished demorphing. I was easily hidden by the forest of tree-trunk legs and tails all around me. All I had to do now was open the lock. Without benefit of fingers.

There were guards now. Now that the trap had been sprung. Six big Hork-Bajir armed to the teeth stood outside and around the cage.

But the entire prison was in the shadow of a sharp escarpment leading up to the weapon. It was maybe fifty feet high, almost vertical. A mound in the center of the scooped-out bowl.

I could see occasional glimpses of Hork-Bajir and Taxxon workers at the top of the slope, but they'd have had to look almost straight down to see us.

A road had been cut into the escarpment, wide enough to accommodate human trucks. We had to go up that road to reach the weapon.

I hawk-walked out the back of the cage. We hawks aren't fast on our talons, but we do know how to walk. I walked right through the gap between the bars.

A Hork-Bajir-Controller looked down at me, puzzled, but then looked away. I looked at him, equally puzzled. Just how was I supposed to get a key from this guy? Walk up and ask him?

Actually . . .

I hawk-walked around behind a toolshed. It's always weird when you find the Yeerks using normal, human stuff. This looked like one of the backyard toolsheds you buy at Sears.

I walked behind the toolshed and I began to morph. The one morph that would seem perfectly at home here.

I morphed Ket Halpak.

I swaggered confidently out from behind the toolshed and walked over to the Hork-Bajir who looked like he was in charge.

"They want to see you," I said.

"Who?"

I jerked my head over my shoulder toward the main building. "They."

It's one of the things you can count on in this world: There's always a *they*.

The Hork-Bajir scowled. The Yeerk in his head was half annoyed, half afraid. "The Visser isn't here yet, is he?"

I turned my head and looked away. Like I wasn't allowed to say more. Now the guy was ten percent annoyed and ninety percent scared.

I held out my claw. "Give me the key."

And it was just that simple. He handed me the key. I walked over and unlocked the cage.

"What are you doing?" one of the other Hork-Bajir-Controllers demanded.

I turned on him and swung my left fist up in a vicious uppercut. It connected with his jaw. He went down.

The remaining four guards hesitated for a split second. Just long enough for Jara Hamee and the others to come tearing out of the cage. I caught sight of something growing fast on the dirt floor of the cage. It was still about halfway mosquito, but there was no mistaking the tail growing out of that bug.

There was a minute of sharp, brutal combat. Five free Hork-Bajir (including myself) against the four guards. Then Ax joined the fight and it all ended quickly.

We shoved and dragged the guards into the cage and locked them up.

Everyone morphed to battle morph. Me, I demorphed. We would need an eye in the sky. I caught a little breeze and floated up, just a dozen feet off the ground. I looked at our little force. Four free Hork-Bajir, a tiger, a wolf, a gorilla, an Andalite, and a very large elephant.

A strange little platoon of warriors.

<The beautiful thing is, they can yell all they

want. The Yeerks will just think they're *our* Hork-Bajir,> Cassie said of the guards in the cage.

<Okay,> Jake said. <So far, so good. But we have a job to do.>

<Ooh, he's getting all John Wayne,> Marco said with a laugh.

Jake ignored the remark. <We have to take that weapon and blow it up. Quiet and fast. We want to be in there before anyone has a chance to react.>

There was a moment of expectant silence.

Then Marco said, <Rachel! What's keeping you>?>

<Oh, I forgot,> she said. And then, in true Rachel style, she yelled, <Let's do it!>

<Thank you,> Marco said. <We can't run off on another idiot suicide mission without the blessings of the always insane Xena, Warrior Princess.>

We formed up and then, on a signal from Jake, they tore out of there, out of concealment, out into the open, racing like mad to reach the weapons platform before something could go wrong.

But I was in the air, and I had my own hawk's eyes. So I could see that already something had gone wrong.

CHAPTER 27

Up the steep road my friends and allies ran. They were directly behind a big dump truck. Mostly invisible to the unsuspecting Yeerks above them.

But they were not invisible. Not to the helicopter that came fwap-fwap-fwapping its way over the trees and into the concealed facility.

It came around and swept low. It was a small helicopter. With one of those bubble canopies just large enough to hold a pilot and one passenger.

One *human* passenger. Nothing else would have fit.

The Hork-Bajir guard had acted as if Visser

Three was expected. This had to be him arriving now.

The sun was on the canopy, blinding, hiding the persons inside. An eagle or an osprey might have been able to see better. They're adapted for looking through sunlight on water. But all I could see was the vague outline of a human form. A finger pointing at my friends. And a flash of a pony-tail.

Aria!

The helicopter roared past, oblivious to me, spinning me roughly in its rotor wash. It disappeared around the far side of the mound.

How could I have been so stupid?

How could I have ever been stupid enough to hope? How could I have failed to know? Had I been blinded by some pathetic desire for normalcy?

It was all an act! Aria, saving the little girl's life, just an act! A show put on for the benefit of any Animorph who might be watching.

I raged at myself. Raged and berated myself, piling anger on top of anger.

Anger was good. Anger was safe. Anger was so much better than the other emotions that threatened to surface and overwhelm me.

<Fool, Tobias! Fool!> I cried. <Every two hours she went back to the bathroom at the hotel. Fool!

How could you, of all people, have missed it? How could you, of all people, Tobias, not know what that meant?>

Two hours! Two hours in *morph*!

A morph! Aria was a *morph*!

I felt sick. I could barely flap my wings. I couldn't think. I couldn't see. Everything was just spinning around me.

I hadn't realized till that moment how much this hope had meant to me. A home. A family.

<Not for you, Tobias, you idiot! You fool! I hate you! I hate you! I want you to die!>

I couldn't fly. I landed hard and lay there in the dirt. I just kept saying it, over and over in my head. <I hate you, Tobias. I hate you. I want you to die.>

In my life as a human, in my life as a bird, I have never been lower than that. I knew my friends were fighting. I knew they needed me. But I couldn't . . .

. . . couldn't.

After a while, a clawed hand snatched me roughly from the ground and I realized I was moving very fast.

"Come with me, Tobias. The weapon is about to explode."

It was Toby. In some distant corner of my mind I wondered how, why she had come. Later I would learn that the battle had gone badly for my friends. It was Toby who'd come to the rescue with the other Hork-Bajir.

She had seen me fall. She saved me. And when we were safe again, she handed me to Rachel.

How did Toby know to give me to Rachel? I don't know. All I know is I was carried, bundled up in Rachel's arms, till we made it back.

They took me to the barn. Cassie looked me over, lifting wings and spreading feathers. Looking for an injury.

"Tobias, where were you hit?" she asked me, puzzled.

I felt like I had to pull the words out of a deep well, like they each weighed a thousand pounds. <I wasn't,> I said.

"Then what's the matter?" Jake asked.

<It's Aria,> I said.

"Your cousin? The woman who wants to take you in?" Jake said.

<She's a morph,> I said without any emotion at all. <It's all a trap. She's Visser Three.> Then I laughed. <The "woman" who was going to be my family? She's Visser Three! Hah, hah, hah! Now, that's funny. That is really, really funny.>

135

CHAPTER 28

I didn't have much time to sit and feel sorry for myself. That would have to come later. I had an appointment.

It was my birthday. I was supposed to hear the last statement left to me by my father. Or my *real* father, whatever that meant.

All a sham, of course. But I had to go through with it. It was a trap, but the only way out of the trap was to step right in.

Aria was Visser Three. She/he had been looking for me. Which meant she/he suspected me. If I didn't show up, the Yeerks would assume I had figured out the trap. They'd assume I was an Animorph.

Why did they suspect me in the first place? Who knew? But it was an easy leap from deciding I, a human boy, was one of the so-called Andalite bandits to guessing that the others were human, too. To guessing that they were kids I had known.

From then on, it would be a deadly chess game with only one possible end.

They would get Jake. He had been my friend.

Jake would be made into a Controller. Even if he died resisting them, they'd move from him to Marco, his best friend, and Rachel, his cousin. From Rachel to Cassie. Game over.

I had to find a way to walk into that lawyer's office and let Visser Three spring his trap. And not get caught.

And worst of all, I had to do it alone. He would have his forces clustered all around De-Groot's office. One glimpse of a strange animal and it would be all over. Visser Three would *know*.

In fact, my friends would have to be somewhere else. While I went in to face DeGroot and the foul fake of Aria, they would go back and launch an attack on the Yeerks, attempting to clean up the weapons site we'd hit earlier.

I morphed to human a long way from the office, just to eliminate any chance of being seen. I walked eight blocks to the lawyer's office. Walked. I hadn't walked that far in a very long time.

It's a lame way to travel. When you fly, you're living in three dimensions. When you crawl the earth like a human, there are just two. It was slow as well. And there were traffic lights and other people and cars and . . . flying was so much better.

So be happy, I told myself bitterly. *It's a good thing you aren't going to be human again. You can still fly.*

No family, but I could fly.

I was shaking and scared by the time I reached the office. It wasn't so much for me. I guess at some level I didn't care all that much if I lived or died right then. I just worried about blowing it somehow. For the others. For my friends.

I guess it's true what they always say about combat soldiers. They may start out fighting for their country, but they end up fighting for the guy next to them in the foxhole.

I didn't so much care about the fate of the human race at that moment. I wasn't human. I was a hawk. But I cared about Jake, and Cassie, and Marco, and Ax-man, and Rachel. Always Rachel.

The receptionist was gone when I walked, trembling, through the door. I stood there, unsure of what to do. Then the two of them came from the inner office.

Aria smiled a big smile. "You must be To-bias," she said.

I remembered seeing her for the first time. Watching her through her window at the hotel, me flying hundreds of feet in the air. Then it struck me. The thing that had bothered me then: Supposedly, she'd been in the African bush for years or whatever. But when she'd left her room, she'd paused to check her hair.

Perfectly appropriate for a normal woman. Just a bit wrong for a woman who spent her days hiding in blinds and racing around in open-topped Land Rovers.

I nodded. "Yeah. I'm Tobias."

My role was tough street kid. It was easy for me to pull off, given that I usually forgot to make facial expressions and had a tendency to stare.

She came and put her arms around me. She hugged me close. The morph that called herself Aria.

Visser Three.

I stiffened and tried to pull away.

"It's okay," she said with perfect sincerity. "Tobias, we're family. I want to take care of you."

DeGroot came over and shook my hand. He said, "Come on in, young man."

If you weren't looking for it, you'd never no-tice it: the way DeGroot stayed back from Aria.

Like she was someone he didn't want to get too close to. Like she was someone he didn't want to touch.

Someone he feared.

So, I thought, *DeGroot is in on this. He's a Controller. He knows who Aria is.*

We all took seats in the office. DeGroot, looking to Aria for cues. Aria, playing the role of concerned, decent woman. Me, being the tough street kid.

One wrong move. One slight wrong move, and Yeerks would pile in on me from directions I hadn't even thought of yet.

"We are here today to carry out the reading of an important document left for Tobias by his father. By . . . by a man different than the man you believed to be your father."

I shrugged. "Whatever."

Aria leaned toward me. "Aren't you interested in finding out who your real father is?"

I laughed. "Did he leave me any money?"

DeGroot's eyebrows shot up. "No."

I rolled my eyes. "Figures."

DeGroot tapped the pages to straighten them. "Then we'll just go straight to reading the document. If that's —"

Some little bit of Visser Three showed through then. "Read it," he/she snapped. Then, forcing a smile, said, "I'm anxious to hear what this is all about."

So the lawyer began to read.

I had forgotten how to use facial expressions. I was used to being a hawk and not a human.

It saved my life.

CHAPTER 29

"Dear Tobias," the lawyer read.

He hesitated, pulled a pair of glasses from his desk, and put them on. Then started again.

"Dear Tobias. I am your father. You never knew me. And I never knew you. I do not know what your life has been over these many years. I hope that your mother found someone else to love. I know that all memory of me has been erased from her mind. All evidence of my time on Earth has been erased."

I could feel Aria staring at me. I could feel her predatory alertness. She was watching my eyes. I did not look at her. She was watching for the twitch that did not come, for the grimace, for the worry, for some emotion that would give me away.

I gave her/him nothing.

"I am being given this opportunity to communicate with you by the very creature who has erased my life on Earth. He has called me back to my duty, and I cannot fail.

"This will all seem very strange to you, my unknown, unseen, unmet son. But I am not one of your people. I have taken on the form of a human, but I am not human."

My lungs wanted to stop breathing. My heart wanted to stop beating. I felt like suddenly everyone, everything was very close in, like Aria/Visser Three was breathing on my cheek, and the lawyer was leaning clear over his desk to whisper his words right in my ear.

Not human!

A reaction! I needed a reaction!

I rolled my eyes and said, "Oh, man," in as sarcastic a tone as I could manage.

The lawyer glanced at Visser Three, then went on.

"I was in a terrible war. I did terrible things. I had to, I suppose. But I grew tired of war, so I ran away. I went and hid among the people of Earth. Among humans. While on Earth, and living as a human, I took the name Alan Fangor."

The lawyer was quoting from memory now, no longer reading. His eyes were narrowed to slits as he watched me.

"I took the name Alan Fangor. But my true name is Elfangor-Sirinial-Shamtul."

Time stopped.

I felt like I'd grabbed hold of a million-volt power line. Every cell in my body was tingling.

Elfangor! My father!

I could not let a flicker of recognition appear. Not a movement. Not a widening of the eyes. Nothing! Nothing!

The lawyer had stopped. Visser Three glared at me with a woman's eyes.

I shrugged. "Is that it?"

I saw Aria's eyes dim. He/she was disappointed. The tension, the electricity, seemed to slowly seep out of the airless cube of an office.

"There's more," the lawyer said, drawing a delayed breath. "But my true name is Elfangor-Sirinial-Shamtul," he repeated, like he couldn't quite believe that name didn't make me jump up and run around the room. "And though you will never know me and we will never meet, I wanted to make sure that you knew my disappearance from your life was not by my choice. I wanted nothing more than to live out my life, loving your mother and loving you as well."

But we did meet, Elfangor, I thought. *We met as you lay dying. Did you know? Did you guess . . . Father? Did you sense, at that last, terrible mo-*

ment when I had to leave you to the murderer who now sits beside me, that I was your son?

Tears! NO! NO! One tear and I would die.

DeGroot looked annoyed now. Let down. He mumbled through the last paragraph of the letter like he had somewhere else to be.

"But I was part of something larger than myself. I had my duty. There was a great evil I had to fight. There were lives I had to try and save. Including yours and your mother's. I am from a race called Andalites. Duty is very important to us. As it is to many, many humans. I cannot say that I love you, my son, because I do not know you. But know that I wanted to love you. Know that, at least.

"It's signed Elfangor-Sirinial-Shamtul, Prince."

I barked out a harsh laugh. "Well, that figures, doesn't it?"

"What figures?" the creature calling itself Aria asked.

"My so-called 'real father' shows up and he's some lunatic. Some idiot. Perfect. So: No money, right?"

"No money," DeGroot confirmed.

I stood up. Aria did, too.

"You really want to take me in, or were you just hoping I was going to inherit something?" I demanded.

145

"I do want to take you in," she said, smiling falsely. "But it may have to wait just a little while. You see, I was suddenly called back to Africa to do some reshooting of . . . of some lions."

I laughed derisively, still the tough street kid. "Great. I have a nut for a father and a fake for a cousin."

I turned my back on them and walked away.

"Tobias," Aria said.

I turned back to face her. "What?"

"I . . . I knew your father. We were, shall we say, on the opposite sides of certain issues. But he was no fool." Suddenly Aria/Visser Three smiled. It was a faraway smile, like she/he was remembering something from long ago. "Prince Elfangor-Sirinial-Shamtul was no fool. And the galaxy will not soon see his like again."

I threw up my hands. "Good grief, you're as crazy as he was."

I walked out and closed the door behind me. I heard DeGroot say, "Shouldn't we take him? Just to be safe? Make him one of us?"

Aria snorted derisively. "He's street trash. A waste of a Yeerk. Elfangor would be ashamed. His son should be a warrior. A worthy adversary, not some young fool. A pity, really."

I'd been in morph for a long time. I left the office and made it to a safe place without being followed or watched. I demorphed. I didn't think about the fact that I'd decided to remain as a human. I demorphed to hawk before I could be trapped.

But then I morphed again. Back to human. See, I wanted to cry. I wanted to cry a lot, for a long time. And hawks don't cry.

CHAPTER 30

I could see it all, now. DeGroot said he had inherited the letter when his father died and he took over the law practice. The younger DeGroot was a Controller. He must have almost had a heart attack when he went through his father's old files and the name Elfangor-Sirinial-Shamtul jumped up at him.

There was not a Yeerk alive who didn't know that name.

Visser Three had wondered what happened to the son of his archenemy. Did Elfangor's son know the truth? Was Elfangor's son somehow connected with the "Andalite bandits" who caused the Visser such pain?

Investigation had revealed that I had disappeared from school and from the custody of my indifferent relatives. That must have really piqued Visser Three's interest.

So he devised a trap. Invent a cousin. Offer me what I obviously did not have: a home. Lower my defenses. Then read me the letter.

But then came the complication: Visser Three had a crisis to deal with. The young Hork-Bajir named Bek. He would need two traps: one for me, one for the free Hork-Bajir.

Just in case I was connected with the "Andalite bandits," he would play the role to the hilt: In that first visit to check out Bek, he pretended to a humanity he did not have. Later he arranged to make it seem he'd saved some girl's life. What better proof that he was truly a human?

It would have worked. Except for the fact that Visser Three was called suddenly to the facility where they had just "captured" a group of free Hork-Bajir.

He'd been passing as Aria at the time. He needed to get to the weapons facility quickly. A helicopter would do the trick, but he would need to travel in human morph.

I saw him. And that was all that saved my life. And doomed his plan.

I flew back to my meadow, my mind and heart more full than I would have thought possible.

Elfangor. My father.

I had no doubt about who had erased Elfangor's life on Earth. Who had allowed him to leave me that one, short letter.

Only the Ellimist could have done it.

I landed back on my favorite branch in my favorite tree. He had left me. My mother never remembered him. He had never existed for her, so she did not feel the pain of it. And I would not have known, but for the letter.

And now, I guess I could be angry at him. But that wasn't how I felt. Elfangor had run away from his duty when he came to Earth. He'd had no choice but to return to that duty. No choice at all, if he was to play the part he had to play, and be the great prince he was.

I'd lost a father. Because of that fact, Elfangor had been where he had to be, when he had to be there, to change the lives of five ordinary kids forever. And maybe . . . *maybe* . . . save the human race.

I wondered why the Ellimist had allowed my father to leave that letter. But I didn't wonder for long. The answer was too simple.

See, I had a duty, too. And who is there to remind you that what you want for yourself is less important than doing what is necessary and right?

<Message received, Father. Message received.>

CHAPTER 31

I swept down across the grass, silent, my wings carefully aligned. I raked my talons forward, flared my tail, swung my wings forward, and dropped with perfect precision.

My talons sank into the back of the rabbit's neck.

And then again, as before, I was not the hawk, but the rabbit. I was not the remorseless killer, I was the victim. Not predator, but prey.

In this vision I felt the pain of my talons in my own neck. I felt the terror of the death from the sky.

But I held on. I had to accept what this vision was telling me. What some corner of my own mind had wanted me to understand.

The rabbit became calm and quiet as I absorbed its DNA. I acquired the rabbit, made it part of me.

Then I tightened my grip till the rabbit stopped squirming. Till its heart stopped beating.

I am, after all, the predator hawk. I kill to eat.

But I am also the human being. And I can never take a life, not even for my own survival, without feeling.

I had heard my father's message come down through the years. Now I heard the message my own mind was telling me: You are both, Tobias. Hawk and human. You always will be. You will always kill to eat. And you will always regret.

It's a rotten situation, I guess. But my duty is to be what I am. A hawk. A boy. Instinct. And emotion. I'll have to go on walking that tightrope.

I ate the mother rabbit. All I could hold.

Then I morphed into the mother rabbit. And I shepherded the babies safely back to their den, as over our heads the other hawk flew, looking down at us for a chance to hunt and eat as I had done.

Life would have been a lot easier for me if I could have been a simple, ruthless animal. If all my decisions were straightforward. If everything made sense.

But that's not the way it is for human beings.

I looked up at the other hawk through terrified

rabbit eyes. I had become prey, this time for real. This is what it felt like. This is what my prey saw when they felt my shadow blot out the sun. It was good that I knew.

<Sorry, my brother hawk,> I said to the shadow of death above me. <There's nothing left for you in this meadow. These little ones are under my protection now.>

I killed to eat. But I didn't need to eat these little ones. These I would save. These little ones I could pity. That was the human thing to do.

That night I went to Rachel's room. She was asleep. She was ticked off when I woke her up. But she rolled out of bed and put on a robe and told me she'd never get any sleep with some idiot bird coming in and out at all hours.

Then she showed me the cake. She lit a candle and I blew it out by flapping my wing. Neither of us sang "Happy Birthday." But she said it.

"Happy birthday, Tobias."

I was getting small. I was getting small very fast.

I've shrunk before, when I've morphed various insects, for example. But this was new. I was shrinking as a human.

The only good thing was that at least my morphing suit was shrinking, too. Bad to be shrinking. Worse to be shrinking right out of your clothes.

"Hey!" I yelled. "What did you do to me?"

<Hah! You glory in your swollen, bloated bulk, human! You dare to defy us! We shall see how bold you are when you are the same size as we. Now you will taste bitter defeat! Now you will feel the sting of eternal humiliation!>

"I don't glory in my . . . Hey, who are you calling bloated? Wait a minute! Stop this!"

I was still shrinking. I'd started at four foot something. Now I was less than a foot tall. And I

was still shrinking. I glanced over and saw a raccoon. He was bigger than I was. Not to mention
being a million times more hostile.

<Cassie!>

I spun around and spotted Tobias, swooping
in like a 747 coming in for a landing.

"Tobias! Look out! They have a shrinking
ray!"

<A what?>

FLASH!

"Never mind. You'll find out soon enough."

<Hah HAH! You all think to resist the might
of the Helmacrons because you are large and because you glow with the transformational power!
But we, too, know how to use the transformational power! Shrink! Shrink! And become our
abject and pitiable slaves!>

<Hey,> Tobias said, sounding puzzled. <I'm
shrinking. And you've already shrunk!>

"Tobias! You have to warn the others not to
come in here! Somehow they're using the power
of the blue box to do this."

<I can't leave you. You're less than six inches
tall!>

"Warn the others!" I cried.

Tobias turned, but he was shrinking fast. He
was already down to about hummingbird size.
Suddenly the door was much farther away for
him.

<Well, this is unfortunate,> he said.

A huge, galumphing form appeared in the doorway: Marco.

"Get back!" I screamed.

But of course what he heard was, "Get back!" FLASH!

"Hey!" Marco yelled. "No flash photography."

<Marco! Quick, before you shrink. Warn the others to stay out!>

"Say what? Before I *what*?"

But he turned and yelled over his shoulder. "Jake! Ax! Rachel! Stay out of here!"

I could see him peering down at me. His face was about the size of the Goodyear Blimp — if it was about to land on top of you.

"Oh, this isn't good," he said.

I was shrinking still further. I was already as small as a cockroach. The roof of the barn already looked like it was the sky. A dim overhead light might as well have been the moon.

Marco was standing on sequoia legs, with feet the size of twin *Titanic*s.

"What's happening in there?" Jake yelled.

"Well," Marco said calmly. "The Helmacrons have the blue box and they seem to be using it in a kind of bizarre way."

"I'm coming in," Jake said decisively.

"No!" Marco yelled in a voice that already sounded like someone breathing helium.

"No, Jake and Ax, do not come in!" Then, as an afterthought, he said, "Rachel, *you* could come in."

<Marco!> Tobias chided.

"Hey, the Wicked Witch gets to be full size and I'm down here singing, 'We represent the Lollipop Guild'? I don't think so."

<Rachel, Jake, everyone stay out!> Tobias cried in thought-speak that we all heard clearly.

"Okay, everyone just stay put," Jake ordered. "Look, the other Helmacron ship took off. Rachel hit it with a brick."

I would have laughed. Only I was now shrinking down to the point where scattered bits of hay on the ground were looking like huge, felled trees. Grains of dirt were the size of soccer balls.

"I think I'm done shrinking!" I said. Not that anyone heard me. Something flew into view. Something that seemed weirdly large. Tobias. He was roughly the size of a very small fly. But he was about as big as me.

<I think I've stopped shrinking,> he said.

"Me, too."

<But we're the same size. I should be smaller than you. I started out much smaller than you.>

"I guess that's not how it works," I said. "I think the idea here is to shrink us all to the same size as the Helmacrons themselves."

Marco, now no more than three inches tall himself, came walking over. He was huge to us. But his face was getting closer all the time.

"Oh, man, you guys are small," he said. "Honey, I shrunk the Animorphs!"

"Rachel! Get a brick!" Jake said in a huge voice that reverberated around us.

ANIMORPHS®

K. A. Applegate

It turns out the Yeerks are not the only invaders of Earth. New intruders, the Helmacrons, are smart, powerful, and no bigger than a grain of sand! They might not be able to fight humans one on one, but they have the technology to shrink other creatures down to <u>their</u> size.

ANIMORPHS #24: THE SUSPICION

K.A. Applegate

COMING IN NOVEMBER!

It's a big battle at the tiniest level.
The Animorphs, the Helmacrons...and Visser Three!

Before the Animorphs...

Dak Hamee
One Hork-Bajir saw the future.

Aldrea
One Andalite lost her family.

Esplin 9466
One Yeerk took control – of everyone.

the hork-bajir chronicles

K. A. Applegate

<It's Here>

ANIMORPHS

1999 Wall Calendar

- Illustrated by the Animorphs cover artist.

- Features a different Animorph each month.

- Includes all the morphs, vital stats, plus—secret messages from the Animorphs!

Mind-blowing Cover that Changes Before Your Eyes!

Watch Animorphs on Television this Fall!